ALLY'S WORLD

KAREN McCOMBIE

TATTOOS, TELLTALES AND TERRIBLE, TERRIBLE TWINS

■SCHOLASTIC

foR MY NeighbOURS COLiN (the REAL COLiN,
aNd his REAL thRee Legs) aNd DeRek
(the REAL DeRek, AND a cat that isN't COLiN)

First published in the UK in 2002 by Scholastic Children's Books
An imprint of Scholastic Ltd
Euston House, 24 Eversholt Street, London, NW1 1DB, UK
Registered office: Westfield Road, Southam, Warwickshire, CV47 0RA
SCHOLASTIC and associated logos are trademarks and or registered
trademarks of Scholastic Inc.

This edition published by Scholastic Ltd, 2006

Text copyright © Karen McCombie, 2002
The right of Karen McCombie to be identified as the author of this work has
been asserted by her.

Cover illustration copyright © Spike Gerrell, 2002

10 digit ISBN 0 439 94285 3
13 digit ISBN 978 0439 94285 0

British Library Cataloguing-in-Publication Data.
A CIP catalogue record for this book is available from the British Library

Printed by Nørhaven Paperback A/S, Denmark
Papers used by Scholastic Children's Books are made from wood grown in
sustainable forests.

1 3 5 7 9 10 8 6 4 2

www.scholastic.co.uk/zone

Contents

PROLOGUE

Dear Mum,
Saw a scan of Sandie's (soon to be) little brother or sister today. She took it out in the middle of McDonald's, which wasn't a *great* idea since it ended up with greasy, salty fingerprint smears all over it once me and our other friends had passed it round the table, cooing.

Actually, not all of us were cooing. Everyone gave Chloe the evil eye when she snorted and said it looked like a fuzzy photo of a doughnut. I mean, yeah – the *first* scan Sandie showed us *did* look a bit like a doughnut, but the baby was only about five minutes old and the size of a ... well, a *dough-nut* at the time. Now *this* fuzzy blob is definitely baby-shaped, with fingers and toes and a slightly startled expression on its face. (You can see the family resemblance already. Whisper "Boo!" from two streets away and Sandie jumps.)

But Sandie's doing pretty OK with the whole baby thing now (after a wobbly, slightly stroppy start). I guess it was just weird at first; you know – being an only child for thirteen years and then this new person is about to come along and you're automatically meant to love it and be all right about the fact that your parents seem to have forgotten your name – never mind your *existence* – they're so excited.

That got us all talking about the pros and cons of being an only child vs having brothers and sisters. Kellie (only child) said she loved having her mum to herself, whereas Kyra (only child) said that was the worst thing about it. The best thing, according to Kyra, was that you're in a better position to get more pocket money. What a surprising thing for Kyra to come out with – *not*. Jen (one older sister) and Chloe (two younger brothers) didn't really have much to say about it, but that was 'cause they were both drooling over the cute guy on till number three. Salma (one older sister, tiny twin sisters, one practically live-in small niece) said she fantasized about being an only child and living in a house where you could put things down and they'd still be there ten minutes later. I think she was talking about the time she found Rosa, Julia and Laurel flushing the contents of her make-up bag down the toilet. Or maybe it was the time she found them posting her brand-new pack of Kotex pads into the video, one by one.

Me? I couldn't imagine life without Tor humming the theme tune to all his favourite animal shows, and how boring would mealtimes be without him constructing the Empire State Building out of peas? And Rowan – life's never dull when you live with someone who changes their hairstyle five times a day and is clinically addicted to glitter*. Linn can be fun, too ... even if it is only for about ten minutes a month.

I know you're an only child, Mum, but after the last couple of weeks, I sometimes found myself wishing that Dad was too. I know that sounds mean, but I think you'll understand when you read this. Just be glad (oh, so glad) that you weren't around when...

Hey, I don't want to spoil my story. Turn the page and it'll all become (horribly) clear...

Love you lots,

Ally

(your Love child No. 3)

* I wouldn't miss Rowan's cooking, though. We had cauliflower and cheese *chilli* tonight: I rest my case.

Chapter 1

BONJOUR! HOLA! HELLO!

"Do you like it?"

Tor and I tilted our heads and studied Rowan's handiwork. On the wall in the kitchen – right next to the cork pinboard (which was so covered in clutter that you couldn't actually *see* the pinboard) – was a poster, surrounded by a frame of plastic bananas, linked together with wire.

"Yeah, it's quite good," I told her.

"Well, how about when I do … *this*!"

And with a flourish, Rowan flipped the switch and illuminated the bananas. (Fairy lights disguised as fruit…)

"Is that where bananas come from?" Tor asked, after he and I had broken into spontaneous applause.

"Croatia?" frowned Rowan, staring at the poster's red-roofed houses and blue bay for clues. "Um, I don't think so. Why?"

Rowan couldn't really see what our little brother was getting at. To her, it was a nice image of an ancient harbour town, and the fairy-light bananas just gave it that extra added something.

"Bet you don't even know where Croatia is!" I grinned at her.

"I do! It's the gateway to central Europe!"

"Ro – you just read that off the poster!"

"Didn't!"

"Did! It's printed right there under the word 'Croatia', hidden behind those bananas!"

"Never noticed that," Rowan shrugged. "So where *is* Croatia, if you're so clever, Ally Pally?"

It's pretty dumb of Rowan to geographically challenge a girl who happens to sleep in the same room as a giant map of the world. And Ro seemed to have forgotten that Croatia was one of the places Mum sent us a letter from not so long ago. *I* remember, 'cause I'd put a red pin in some town called Zadar (the postmark on the front of the envelope) when the letter arrived earlier in the year.

"It's in-between Slovenia and Serbia," I told her.

Rowan's eyes glazed over with confusion. Good grief, did she daydream her way through Geography and General Studies when they talked about Yugoslavia and the war there? Um, probably, knowing Ro.

"*Or*," I tried again, "look at Northern Italy on

the map, then turn right. That's the general direction for Croatia."

"Uh-huh... OK, so who wants to blow up the donkey?" said Rowan, absently.

"Yeah, me!" shrieked Tor, tearing through into the hall (where there were giant fake sunflowers in the vase; party streamers dangling from the roof; plastic flowery garlands wrapped all around the bannisters and an old beach towel pinned down where the welcome mat used to be).

Rowan may score nil points for her knowledge of modern history, but she's a star pupil when it comes to cheering people up (me, in particular). I'm not normally the jealous type, but I *had* come over slightly miserable yesterday, thanks to the fact that Billy, Jen, Chloe and Kyra were all jammy enough to be jetting off abroad this summer, and even Sandie, Kellie and Salma were going to be visiting relatives in places that weren't very far but certainly weren't *here*. Which is where *I* was going to be, along with the rest of my skint family.

I hadn't moaned to Dad about it, of course – I knew he worked really hard and couldn't help it if his bike shop hadn't exactly made him a millionaire, or even rich enough to close the shop and schlep away with us and a tent for a couple of weeks somewhere. (Although he *was* closing the shop for four days next week, to go to this big bike fair thing in Yorkshire somewhere. But still, that was yet *more* work and *no* play.)

Anyway I did find myself moaning a bit to Rowan – and next thing I know, she's raiding the cupboards and wangling a little bit of cash out of Dad to transform the house into a holiday-haven-cum-carnival. This morning – instead of our usual Saturday morning jaunt to the pet shop – me and Tor joined Rowan in scouring every pound shop in Wood Green and ended up coming back here with mountains of summery tat, which we spent ages fixing up around the place.

Best of all was the holiday posters Rowan blagged for free from the travel agents on Crouch End Broadway. As well as the banana-customized poster of Croatia in the kitchen, we'd stuck a poster up on the door of each room to give it a theme, so now the living room was Spain (it had a drawing of a big yellow sun, the same colour as the living room walls), Tor's room was Australia (it had a koala on it), the loo was the Danube (nice water theme), Dad's room was the Seychelles (figured he deserved some luxury), Rowan's room was Nepal (not that she'd know where that was), mine was Hawaii (cool blue skies) and Linn's was Iceland, which spoke for itself, but wouldn't last long once she saw it, we didn't think.

"Fancy helping me hang up my sign, Ally?" Rowan asked, grabbing a bundle of stuff off the table, which was now covered in a multicoloured plastic tablecloth (£2.99) with an interesting design featuring surfboarders, stripy umbrellas and pineapples.

"Sure," I nodded, grabbing a chair for Rowan to stand on, and slowly following her to the front door. (The stupid torn ligaments in my ankle weren't quite up for speed-walking, stepladders or can-can dancing quite yet.)

Passing the living room, I could see Tor gently turning purple, as he panted air into the giant inflatable donkey-headed rubber ring (a bargainous £1.99 from Ahmed's *very* super Superstore) that was now going to take over from the beanbag as his TV-viewing seat for the summer. But from the way the dogs were bouncing around barking (Rolf) and growling (Winslet) at the rapidly expanding donkey, I wasn't sure if the thing would last too long without fangs spoiling the fun.

"Hold these," said Rowan, passing me a hammer and nails as she opened the door and clambered up on the chair she'd grabbed from me. "So, have you heard from that boy?"

That Boy … that would be Feargal, who I'd been out with once (last Sunday) on a not-quite-date. Big success *that* was, since he'd not-quite-phoned me ever since. Yet *another* reason to get the summertime blues…

"Ro, is your hair darker?" I squinted up at her, ignoring her awkward question and passing her the hammer and a nail.

How weird; sunlight tends to make most people's hair lighter – even Joanne, the Chinese girl in my class, says the sun turns her black hair dark brown – but in Rowan's case, nature was playing tricks. Her longish wavy hair was normally browny-brown, same as mine (and Dad's and Tor's), but out here in the daylight, I'd definitely describe it as…

"Deep Oak. That's what it said on the packet. Do you like it?" Rowan beamed down at me, as she fixed some windchimes to the door frame.

With that name, I was worried that my sister might have accidentally dyed her hair with floor varnish. But whether it was that or genuine, salon-tested hair gloop, the main problem was obvious.

"Ro!" I squeaked. "Grandma will *kill* you! You know she hates anything fake!"

Like hair dye, like tattoos, like piercings, like cosmetic surgery. Our gran is pretty laid-back in many ways (temporary stuff like make-up and fashion she can live with, as long as she can get to tut at it) but not when it comes to any of the above.

"I know – but I really want to have black hair, like Von!"

Von: one of Ro's two best buddies, who both have dyed hair, tattoos and piercings; who are both regarded with serious caution by Grandma.

"She's definitely going to kill you!" I warned my sister.

"Ah, but not if I do it gradually, so she doesn't notice! I mean, this colour – it's only one shade up from what I am normally!"

Yeah, *right*.

And the rest. That was like saying it's nearly Christmas in the middle of July...

But try telling Rowan something when she's made up her style-wise mind.

"You're squint," I pointed out instead, watching Rowan's handmade sign lurch to one side and clatter into the untinkly windchimes.

"Better?" she asked, pulling up one side of the green twine.

"*Bella, bella!*" came a voice, at the same time as the gate creaked open.

"Thank you, Stanley," Rowan smiled at Grandma's

boyfriend, as he stood to one side and gestured for our gran to go first. "Do you like it, Grandma?"

Poor Grandma – she pursed her lips and looked like she was struggling to say something positive. The most arty, messy thing in her flat is the photo of us lot (Linn excepted) on her window sill, and now here she was, faced with a set of windchimes constructed by Rowan from a pack of coloured, transparent picnic forks from Woollies, and a sign done up in looky-likey mosaic (painted, dried macaroni) that said "El Paradiso". Our gran was obviously dumbstruck, and she hadn't even *seen* the inside yet.

"Is your hair darker?" she frowned instead at Ro.

"No!" Rowan lied. "It just needs to be washed!"

"You need your *brain* washed!" Linn called out, walking down the pavement towards the house, still amazingly quick with a sarky comment, even after a hard day's work at the clothes shop. "What exactly are you *doing* to our house?"

"Transforming it into a holiday haven! El Paradiso!" I butted in cheerfully, before Ro's hackles rose and the two of them started hissing at each other. "You were there when Rowan asked Dad about it last night, remember, Linn?"

"Yeah, but I didn't know she'd planned on making our home look like a Primary One art project!"

Hmm… Linn hadn't seen the inside of the house either. Seemed like so far it was three to two in favour of El Paradiso. (Stanley's opinion didn't count since, technically, he wasn't quite family.)

"Dad!" called out Tor, his spooky antennae making him leap to his feet and come running out of the house to meet our dad before any of the rest of us noticed him approaching.

"Hi," said Dad flatly.

"Are you OK?" I asked him, thinking he'd taken one look at the sign and wanted us to move before the neighbours called the style police.

He didn't say anything. He had the stunned look of someone who'd just realized they'd washed their jeans with a twenty pound note in the pocket. Either that or he'd seen a ghost.

"Martin?!" said Grandma loudly, in the tone of voice she uses when she catches us watching *The Weakest Link* instead of doing our homework.

"Um, sorry, sorry…" Dad shook his head, like he'd just woken up from a coma. "I've just had the strangest phone call…"

"Strange? *How* strange?" I asked him, feeling a small knot of panic twist in my stomach.

"Well, no – not *strange* exactly, just unexpected, I guess," Dad said quickly, spotting the alarm in my saucer-shaped eyes.

Unexpected…

Call me pessimistic, but I still didn't like the sound of that one little bit.

Chapter 2

(NOT SO) MYSTERIOUS VISITORS...

"This place looks nuts!"

I'm pretty sure Sandie meant that in a good way. She's a huge fan of my family and our foibles (weird word, but then it's a weird family).

"Wow!" she exclaimed, flopping down on the deckchair beside the sofa and gazing up at the huge stained-glass-style sun that was taking up most of the living-room window.

"Nice, isn't it?" I grinned, pointing towards the sun (the fake one, not the real one, although that was out there somewhere beyond the windowpane). "Rowan made it out of these sheets of coloured plastic."

The daylight pouring through the yellow plastic turned the room even *more* yellow than it already was, giving it a totally tropical feel. "Looks jaundiced," Grandma mumbled when she checked it out ten minutes ago, just before Sandie turned up.

"Wish I could do stuff like this in *my* house," Sandie sighed, kicking her shoes off and making herself right at home. "Mum and Dad would flip out if I tried to stick up something like that in our front room!"

True. Mr and Mrs Walker have the dullest, most traditional house in the universe – apart from Sandie's room, of course, with those giant, mutant pink daisies that me and her painted on the walls one Sunday when her parents were out. They nearly had her adopted once they set eyes on that.

Maybe that's why Sandie's mum and dad were quite happy for her to come and stay with me for a week, while they got their place totally done up before the baby was born. Perhaps they were worried that she'd end up persuading the decorators to do subversive stuff like hang the wallpaper upside down or fit portholes in all the doors or something.

Whatever, a couple of minutes ago she dumped one super-huge holdall outside in our hallway – which helped with the house's overall holiday theme, I guess.

"Ally! And Sandie!" I heard Dad call through from the kitchen. "Tea's nearly ready. Do you girls want to come through? I just want to have a bit of a chat with everyone!"

"Ooh, it must be about your visitors! How exciting!"

"Yeah..." I replied dubiously, stepping over the

donkey ring and a conked-out Rolf, who was doing an impression of a semi-live bearskin rug.

To be honest, I wasn't sure what I thought about these visitors. I'd tried to scrutinize Dad's face for clues when he told us about the phone call he'd just taken from his long-lost brother back at the shop, but it seemed to register more blank shock than bolt-out-of-the-blue pleasant surprise, which wasn't too promising.

"What're your uncle and aunt like?" asked Sandie, following me through to the kitchen.

"Can't remember," I told her truthfully.

I was four when my uncle Joe and his wife emigrated to Canada. I have a *few* memories from around that age – like being sick on my dad when he played aeroplanes with me over his head, and watching six-year-old Rowan go hysterical after idly ramming Barbie's sandal up her nostril and jamming it there – but I've got no memories at all of Uncle Joe and Auntie Pauline. "We never saw that much of them," I remember Mum once telling me. "Your dad and his brother are like chalk and cheese. There wasn't a problem; they just didn't have much in common, and drifted apart over the years."

They drifted apart all right. Oceans apart, once Uncle Joe jaunted off to Canada. Apparently, Dad had tried writing loads of times (phoning was a bit too expensive), but Uncle Joe never got round to replying, and Dad's letters petered out in the vacuum. For most of the time, it's been a case of exchanging a lone Christmas card once a year. In his, Dad's always written a little note to say how we're all doing. In Uncle Joe's, all there is is a "Happy Doodah" type message that they send to everyone, plus an up-to-date photo of his kids – nine-year-old twins called (wait for it) Carli and Charlie. Actually, there's always a scuffle between me, Linn, Ro and Tor when Uncle Joe's card arrives, simply because – if you want to know the ugly truth – we're all dying to see how much weirder-looking our Canadian cousins have got one year on. I mean, take babies: they're usually round and blobby and cute, right? Not our cousins. Just months old, they looked more like bad-tempered elves than anything else. And time hasn't done them any favours; they get just a little bit bigger, a little bit elfier with every passing year...

That's so rotten of me to say, I know. Maybe they stood staring unsmiling at the camera because they hated getting their picture taken. Maybe they were really nice and friendly (and not so elfy) when you got to meet them in the flesh.

Well, I'd be finding out pretty soon. In about eighteen hours, to be exact.

"Still, I think it's *very* odd to travel halfway around the world without letting you know he was coming!" Grandma was saying to Dad, as he settled down on a chair at the kitchen table.

Despite it being Rowan's turn to make tea (she was just serving up an amazingly edible mix of salad-type stuff, plus – eek! – a bowl of cold Spaghetti Hoops), the table, laid out with paper plates, plastic cutlery and glasses complete with jaunty cocktail umbrellas, was a pretty popular place to be this evening. Dad was plonked at one end, surrounded by Linn, Rowan, Grandma and Stanley, who was becoming something of a regular fixture round ours. Which was fine – he's a really nice bloke, apart from clumps of white hair that stick out of his ears, but it's not like he can really help that. (Though shouldn't barbers do a nose and ear hair-trim service? They could do specials: "Free ear trim with every cut and blow dry!")

Apart from those five, there was a chair and an old stool set aside for me and Sandie. At first I couldn't see Tor – and then I caught a glimpse of the top of his head. He was sitting (just above floor level) on another of our saggy, stripy deckchairs, which he must have dragged in from the garden to solve the chair-shortage problem. Rolf (if he ever woke up) and Winslet were going to *love* that – he was a perfect height to feed them snacklets off his plate without Grandma's stern disapproval spoiling the fun.

"Irene –"

(It's always very strange to hear Grandma called anything other than "Grandma".)

"– once my brother gets something in his head, there's nothing much you can do to stop him," Dad explained, leaning forward and helping himself to the food. "He probably thought it'd be an excellent idea to turn up and surprise us – like something off a TV show!"

"But doesn't he think for a minute that it might not be a convenient time for you?" Grandma continued, frowning. "And I mean, it isn't, is it? You're off to that important bike fair next Wednesday, aren't you?"

Grandma (and her kitten Mushu) were going to be moving in with us from Wednesday to Saturday, to make sure we all ate properly and that Rolf and Winslet didn't have any wild parties for all the neighbourhood dogs while Dad was away.

"Well, I think I'll have to ditch that plan now," Dad shrugged fatalistically. "I can't exactly go swanning off when this is the one chance I get to see Joe in years. And another thing; I kind of need your help over the next couple of weeks, guys…"

Dad gazed around the table, his eyes resting specifically on me, Rowan, Linn and Tor.

"Help how?" asked Linn.

"Well, I can't exactly afford to shut the shop for days on end while Joe and everyone are here, but what I thought I'd do is call Rory – he was going to cover for me going to the bike fair. If he's not too busy I'll see if he can swap things around and let me have a couple of days off this week and a couple of days off next week instead."

"You mean you want *us* to look after Uncle Joe and Auntie Pauline and our cousins for the rest of the holiday?" said Rowan, probably already planning an exciting timetable of craft-related activities for the twins.

"Not exactly; not *all* the time." Dad shook his head. "I'm sure Joe's family have things they want to do and places they want to visit. But on the days I *do* have to work, if you kids wouldn't mind helping entertain Carli and Charlie a little bit, that would be great. And if they're anything like their dad, they'll like a good laugh..."

"Hey, didn't Uncle Joe once put your details in a Lonely Hearts ad without you knowing?" Linn asked, taking the coloured-paper umbrella out of her glass so that she could drink her orange juice without poking her eye out.

Good grief, I'd forgotten about that story. Dad (aged sixteen) knew nothing about it till he got a sackful of mail from women desperate to share his "luxury bachelor penthouse" and help him polish his "top of the range red Porsche". Thanks to Joe's "hilarious" prank, loads of lonely and easily impressed thirtysomething women thought they were writing to a self-made paper-clip tycoon, not a teenage boy who lived in a council house with his mum, his annoying big brother and a rickety second-hand bike as his only form of transport.

"Yes, he did," Dad nodded, with a roll of his eyes.

"And didn't he get expelled from school for locking the music teacher in the cupboard when she went in to find the maracas?" I butted in, dredging up another old story from my memory banks.

"Yep," said Dad. "And then he took off the tape of *Peer Gynt* she'd been playing to the class and put on the Sex Pistols' 'God Save The Queen' instead."

Dad was actually smiling as he recounted that particular misdeed, but I think that's because he's a bit of a fan of punk music himself. And I guess some of Uncle Joe's practical jokes seem funnier in hindsight than they were at the time.

"When you and Melanie got married – didn't Joe stand up and recite a rude limerick at the reception?" Grandma asked.

"Yes, Irene – that was Joe," Dad admitted. "I'm sorry that the one time you met him he was on his worst behaviour."

"What was the limerick?" I found myself asking.

"Never you mind, Ally. I just hope he's grown out of that silly behaviour," said Grandma, disapprovingly. (Couldn't you just have guessed that "Practical Jokes" are firmly on Grandma's list of Things She Doesn't Approve Of? I think they come somewhere between "Eating With Your Mouth Open" and "G-Strings".)

"Well, maybe being a parent has made him more sensible," Dad suggested. "But I wouldn't bet on it. Remember, this is the guy who wore a revolving bow tie at his *own* wedding."

Apparently, the vicar had got very cross, telling Uncle Joe that he wasn't taking the ceremony seriously and that he wouldn't carry on till Uncle Joe had switched his tie off.

"This should be an interesting visit…" Linn frowned. "So where are they going to be staying?"

"Well, that's what I wanted to talk to you all about."

Dad looked edgy. One hand was absently ruffling his short dark hair into mussed-up spikes; a nervous tic of his that's always a dead giveaway.

"So?" Rowan prompted him.

"So, they're coming to stay here."

As Dad spoke, he fixed his eyes firmly on the table, instead of glancing around at us all.

"Here?" Linn barked. "Here *where*? There's only just enough room for *us* in this place! Why can't they stay in a hotel like normal people?"

I knew what Linn was thinking – she was just as curious as the rest of us to meet our remote relatives, but for her, our house was chaotic enough without trying to shoehorn another entire family in between us and the army of pets.

"They *were* booked into a hotel, but I thought *this* way, it'd give us more of a chance to get to know each other. And the only place they'd managed to get at this time of the year was one of those rip-off B&Bs round Victoria that charge a fortune for a room the size of our garden shed," Dad shrugged. "I couldn't let them stay there – so I told them to come and bunk up with us."

"Speaking of sheds – I hope they realize that's where they're going to be sleeping!" said Linn, sticking her thumb in the direction of the garden.

She loves Dad like mad, but I think she despairs of his ditziness sometimes.

"Like a holiday cabin!" came an enthusiastic voice from (nearly) under the table.

"No, Tor, we can't let them sleep out in the

garden shed," Dad shook his head. "That's why I thought we should sit down and talk about how we can do this."

"Maybe we could clear out the attic cupboard – the twins could sleep in there. We could make it all cosy by chucking material over all the boxes and putting a little lamp, or some fairy lights in there!" said Rowan, her eyes gleaming at the opportunity of doing more inventive housey makeovers. "And Carli and Charlie should be small enough not to bump their heads on those low beams!"

"Small – like elves..." I heard Tor mutter to himself.

(I ducked my head under the table to see what he was up to, and spotted him crossed-legged on the deckchair, spearing Spaghetti Hoops off his plate with the spiky end of his cocktail umbrella. Winslet was hunkered down on the floor beside him, ready to pounce on any stray hoops.)

"And where do you suggest Uncle Joe and Auntie Pauline sleep, Ro?" Linn flashed her eyes at our sister. "Standing up in the broom cupboard?"

When you listen to some of her less thought-out suggestions, it can seem like Rowan has the brain of a particularly tiny bird and Linn is always keen to be the first one to point that out to her. But whatever, it *was* going to be a tight squeeze. How could three adults, three sisters, two cousins, a small brother and a Sandie all fit into our animal-infested zoo-cum-home?

"Nobody will be sleeping in any cupboards, or sheds, or tree houses, or whatever else," said Grandma firmly, accompanied by Stanley vehemently shaking his head in support. "There's got to be a sensible solution to this. And you children have to appreciate that your dad hasn't seen his brother for a long, long time, and I'm sure it's very important to him that you're all on your best behaviour when they arrive!"

I noticed Sandie twitching by my side, practically desperate to put her hand up and tell Grandma that she'd be good. I don't think she could believe her luck: up until a couple of days before she thought she'd be hanging around her place watching paint dry, and now here she was in the midst of a proper family saga.

"Thanks, Irene," Dad said with a certain amount of relief in his voice. Grandma's a great referee, and even if she might not have thought much of our uncle on the one occasion she met him, she'd still give him the benefit of the doubt, and make sure we did the same.

"So, let's see," Grandma began, applying her ferociously logical brain to our housing problem.

"For a start, the little boy can share with Tor, and—
Rowan!"

At that very moment, Ro had leant across the table, catching Grandma's eye as she reached out for the enticing bowl of cold Spaghetti Hoops.

"Oh, sorry, Grandma," she began. "I just wanted some more of the—"

But the problem wasn't anything to do with rudeness or Spaghetti Hoops – it was to do with the heart-shaped garland of roses that was now peeking out from under the short sleeve of Rowan's pink T-shirt.

"Oh, *that*!" Ro exclaimed, as if it was the very first time she'd noticed the tattoo. "It's OK, Grandma – it's only a fake! It'll wash off in the shower!"

"It had better, young lady!" said Grandma, staring at my sister over the top of her gold-rimmed specs.

"Grandma, it's just a fashion thing. You *know* I'd never get a *real* tattoo!"

Tomorrow, we'd be seeing first-hand if there was any family resemblance between my dad and his prank-playing brother. But for the first time, I spotted a family resemblance between me and Ro that'd I'd never noticed before: a slight twitch at the side of her mouth. Could it be that she'd just told a porky-pie there?

Secret hair dyes and blatant lies ... what exactly was Rowan up to?

LATE-NIGHT MUNCHIES AND MEMORIES

It's hard to tiptoe down the stairs for a midnight snack when three nosey cats and a slobbery dog are following you in the hope of something interesting happening that involves crumbs.

"Go back to sleep!" I whispered pointlessly at them, as I passed Dad, Tor and Rowan's rooms on the first-floor landing.

One word (OK, four words) from me, and the pets did exactly what they pleased, which was to carry on padding after me, like I was the Pied Piper of Palace Heights Road.

The midnight-snack idea (whatever I could find that wasn't cold Spaghetti Hoops) was actually a bit of a peace offering. Since Sandie's week-long stay at our place had just been reduced to a one-night stay, I felt kind of obliged to make it a good one.

"You can still come over loads when my uncle and his family are here!" I'd tried to say enthusiastically, when I was giving Sandie a magazine makeover in my room (i.e., using all the free make-up I'd collected off the front of mags). "You can help us look after them!"

"Oh, yes, please!" Sandie's big, blue eyes had lit up.

"You know, you can *still* stay!" I'd told her, crumpling with guilt in the face of her blatant niceness. "You heard what Dad said at teatime – that we'd manage somehow!"

Yeah, not wanting to turf Sandie out, Dad had said that – but you could tell Grandma was biting her lip at the impracticality of it all. Then when Sandie had voluntarily offered to go back home (to the dust-sheets, to her parents arguing over which shade of beige to paint the walls), Grandma's shoulders practically sank with relief.

"No, it's fine! I really don't mind!" Sandie had blinked her purple-mascara'd eyelashes at me. (I should have done them blue, to match her eyes and her – I kid you not – *Little Mermaid* PJs.)

Ten out of ten to Sandie for being selfless and thoughtful (and zero out of ten to her mum for buying her naff PJs). But it's a lowly one out of ten to me for feeling slightly *peeved* at Sandie's selflessness and thoughtfulness, since it meant that I'd suddenly ended up being nominated as the person most likely to have Carli as a room-mate.

"Well, she *is* nearest you in age!" Grandma had pointed out, as Rowan and Linn both did that shoulders-sinking-in-relief thing...

The thing is, having an unknown cousin to stay for one night *could* be interesting, but for two whole weeks? That was *scary*. I mean, Carli could be the sweetest girl in the world, and by the end of the two weeks I might be sobbing on the doorstep wishing she could stay for ever. But thinking of that stern little elfin face, I dreaded the fact that this might seem like the longest fortnight in the entire history of the world.

"God, not you too!" I murmured at the top of the last flight of stairs, as Winslet came thundering up from the hall to join the gang.

It was then that I spotted the light shining out from under the living-room door. Had Dad nodded off again in front of some late-night film? I don't know why he bothers – he gets all excited when he reads about a good movie in the paper, and then zonks out before the opening titles are over. Usually he wakes up at something o'clock in the morning, with a stiff neck from falling asleep in a weird position (i.e. slumped sideways with a cat on his head), and has to drag himself to bed. But sometimes one of us – on a middle-of-the-night wee mission – will spot the light on, and go and shoo the cat off Dad's head and shake him into consciousness.

Looked like that was what I was going to have to do now...

"Dad?" I said softly, pushing the living-room door open and tiptoeing inside. Not that there was any point in speaking softly and tiptoeing: Dad was (amazingly) wide-eyed and wide awake.

"Hey, Ally Pally!" he turned and smiled broadly as soon as he saw me.

Dad's smiles; they have the habit of making you feel like you are the *exact* person he most wants to see in the world at that precise moment.

I padded barefoot towards him (followed by a scratchy clawed patter of tiny padded feet, as the procession of pets followed me inside) and leant on the back of the armchair, staring down at the photo album he was holding.

"What are you doing?" I asked.

Duh ... looking at photos, maybe? Perhaps I was more tired than I thought.

"Just flicking through these old photos of Joe," he murmured, pointing at one in particular of two little boys – one gawky and cute, one chubby and cheeky-faced.

They were both in smart clothes (they were pageboys at some cousin's wedding), but while my gawky, cute, eight-year-old Dad smiled a good-as-gold, gap-toothed smile at the camera, his chubby, cheeky-faced, twelve-year-old brother Joe had his eyes crossed, his tongue shoved between his bottom teeth and his lower lip and was holding two fingers up at the back of my dad's head.

"Check this!" Dad laughed, fast-forwarding to a photo taken at Mum and Dad's (very small) wedding.

There they are – Mum (in a long, hippy dress, a bump that was Linn and daisy bouquet), Dad (in a second-hand, 1960s, tight black suit), their parents and a few close friends pictured right after they'd come out of the registry office. They didn't have a professional photographer; just one camera being passed around. And in this particular snap – taken by who knows who – there was everyone, smiling and laughing, except Uncle Joe, crossing his eyes, shoving his tongue between his bottom teeth and lower lip and holding two fingers aloft behind the groom's head.

"Didn't he put a whoopee cushion under your bum after you'd done your speech?" I suddenly remembered, from some story Mum had told me about the reception party back at their flat.

"Yeah – and he nearly got a glass of fake champagne over his head for doing that!" Dad grinned at me.

You know something? Although he was grinning, Dad still seemed slightly shell-shocked to me.

"Dad..."

"Ally..." he mimicked my wary tone.

"Are you looking forward to seeing Uncle Joe?" I asked him, slipping my arm around his shoulders.

As if they sensed my concern, Rolf flopped his hairy head on Dad's feet and a cat that wasn't Colin (Fluffy, in fact) jumped up on one arm of the chair and rubbed herself against Dad's shoulder. Or maybe Fluffy was just hovering around, impatiently waiting for Dad to nod off so she could snuggle down on that warm head of his.

"I guess I am. I mean, apart from you guys, he is my only relation," Dad shrugged.

It was true. When it comes to grandparents, mine are in pretty short supply. My mum's dad – Grandma's husband – died a few years ago, but he was pretty ill and everything, and a lot older than Grandma, so it was sad but kind of good for him, 'cause he didn't have to feel poorly any more. But at least I remember my Grandad Miller; my dad's dad skedaddled right after he was born and my Granny Love went and died when I was little, which wasn't much fun for us kids, since we'd have liked to have known at least one person who was responsible for our lovely dad. *And* his brother Joe...

"Granny Love looks happy there," I mused, pointing to the wedding photo and the shy, smiley woman in the navy trouser-suit standing next to Dad (and his comedy rabbit ears, courtesy of Uncle Joe). Even though I didn't remember her, she looked familiar, just because her thick brown hair, brown eyes and apple-cheeks-as-soon-as-you-smile can be spotted in Dad's face, Rowan's face, Tor's face and my own reflection in the mirror.

"Yeah, she *was* happy," Dad smiled (an identikit Granny Love smile) as he patted my back gently. "But I tell you what would make her happy now."

"What's that?"

"If me and your Uncle Joe could be good friends. I think she was always disappointed that we fought so much when we were little and then just drifted apart once we both left home."

He looked so thoughtful for a split-second that I didn't know the right words to say. Luckily, he started speaking again almost instantly.

"So, anyway, what are you doing up this late, Ally Pally?"

"Peanut-butter sandwiches," I grinned at him. "And chocolate digestives, if there're any left."

"Go on, then!" Dad laughed, pushing me away. "Don't keep Sandie waiting for her midnight snack!"

"Do you want anything?" I asked him, walking towards the door.

"No – I'm heading for bed in a sec," said Dad, snapping the photo album closed. "But I meant to say, thanks for being so good about your cousins coming and everything. I knew I could rely on you."

"It's OK..." I smiled, backing away shyly as I felt my face flushing with pride.

"Oh, and Ally, I meant to ask—"

"Yes?" I said, pausing at the door, with my faithful following of pets, excited all over again at the movement towards the kitchen.

"That *is* just a temporary tattoo that Rowan has, isn't it?"

"Yes, of course!" I told him.

It was only once I'd walked down the chilly, darkened hallway towards the kitchen that my mouth started twitching...

WELL, *ALOHA!*

I ran to the phone, my belly flipping like a pancake (not pleasant to imagine and not a pleasant sensation, I can tell you). But just like every call over the last few days, this one *wasn't* from Feargal.

Boo…

In fact I could hardly hear who it was, Linn was clattering the hoover around so loudly on the stairs above me, giving the house one last suction before our visitors arrived. (Which would be any minute now, unless they'd got stuck in traffic coming from Heathrow.)

"So, what happened to you, Ally?" I could just make out Billy's voice demanding. "I sat waiting for so long that one of the park keepers came over and asked if I was all right. I think he thought I was a homeless teenage runaway!"

"Billy, homeless teenage runaways don't tend to have manicured white poodles with diamanté collars," I grinned into the receiver, sticking my hand over my ear to hear him better. "So what did this guy do? Did he just walk right over and start talking to you?"

"Well, no – he was emptying the bin next to our bench."

"Our" bench, 'cause that's where we always meet. It's not like there's a plaque with our names on it or anything, although that's a cool idea. *Ally and Billy's Bench – Keep (Your Bum) Off*: it has a certain ring to it, doesn't it?

"And what did the park guy say exactly?" I asked.

"He said, 'All right?'"

"Well, I *could* be wrong here, Billy, but it sounds like he was probably just emptying the bin and saying 'All right'. I don't think he was all set to call Social Services about you."

"I guess," sighed Billy, now that his dramatic bubble had deflated. "But why didn't you come?"

"Sorry – I *did* try to phone, but you'd left already. I couldn't come 'cause we're doing a massive clear-up here; we've got my uncle, aunt and cousins from Canada coming to stay today."

"You never said!" Billy mumbled accusingly, as if I was making the whole thing up to get out of our usual Sunday get-together. As *if*... Sundays aren't the same without an hour's worth of Billy drivel to entertain me.

"I never said anything before, 'cause we didn't find out ourselves till yesterday. And we were all in laundry hell this morning."

It was a phone call from Grandma earlier today that alerted Dad to the fact that we really needed to try and get a few roughly matching sets of bedding together so that our relatives didn't end up snoozing under one musty sleeping bag and the fuzzy doggy blanket from Winslet's basket. After that chat, Dad sounded the alarm, and while *he* headed off on the tube to Heathrow (to act as welcoming committee and navigator for the hire-car journey back to our place), me, Linn, Rowan, Tor and Sandie were raiding cupboards, stuffing the washing machine, airing spare quilts and pillows and mending leaky lilos with bicycle puncture-repair kits.

Actually, it was just the *one* leaky lilo; that's what Tor was going to be sleeping on while cousin Charlie got pride of place in Tor's bed (hoped he liked soft toys as much as Tor – he'd be sharing his sleeping hours with a motley collection of cuddly alligators, aardvarks and sloths). I'd be on the blow-up mattress we used when Sandie came for sleepovers, while Carli got *my* bed (hoped she liked company – she'd be sharing her sleeping hours with a motley collection of cats, dogs and little brothers). Uncle Joe and Auntie Pauline were going to get Dad's room, and Dad? Dad was stepping into the hallowed ground of Linn's room...

Yep, it had been decided last night that it would make sense for Linn to move in with Grandma for the two weeks our visitors were with us. It was going to be weird, not having Linn at home, but then she was working all day anyway – her Saturday job at the clothes shop on Crouch Hill had turned into a six-week holiday job. She'd still be coming home for tea in the evenings, so that would feel normal. But how bizarre was it going to be not to have her around in the mornings, sighing over sticky marmalade jars, moaning about soggy towels left on the bathroom floor and growling at toothpaste gloops on the taps?

You know, something told me Linn was going to have a *lovely* time at Grandma's and not miss messy old us one tiny bit...

"So how long are these relatives of yours staying?" Billy asked.

"A fortnight. You can come over and meet them later if you like."

"Fffnnnaarr! *That'll* be right!"

Somehow, I guessed from Billy's snort that hanging out with my extended family sounded about as tempting as supergluing his nostrils closed.

"What's wrong with them?" I asked defensively, although I didn't know what was right *or* wrong with them myself yet.

"Nothing. It's just that I've got aunts and uncles of my own to hang out with, and *that's* boring enough. Why would I want to hang out with yours?"

Not everyone found the idea of my overseas relatives as mind-numbingly dull as Billy did. Right now, two deeply inquisitive friends of mine were lounging about in our kitchen, making the place look untidy, as they waited to meet The Other Loves...

"Got to go – Sandie and Kyra are here. I'll call you later, yeah?"

"Yeah, call me in two weeks' time, when they've gone!"

I said my byes loudly (Linn was thunking the hoover at ear level on the stairs now) and clattered the receiver back in its place on the hall table.

I found my way back into the kitchen barred by a huge, green, swaying swathe of material.

"Now fold it. No – the *other* way!" I heard Sandie tell Kyra.

Bless 'em, at least they were *trying* to be helpful

(had to be Sandie's idea), but instead of putting away the laundry it seemed more like they were trying to make a giant origami swan out of the duvet cover.

I stepped in at Kyra's end, taking hold of the tangled bedding and shooing her back to the table. Kyra may be many things (don't get me started) but practical isn't one of them.

"Was that your uncle on the phone?" asked Sandie, saucer-eyed, from the other end of the duvet. "Are they held up somewhere?"

Her huge bag — barely unpacked before it was zipped shut again, was leaning against the leg of the kitchen table, I noticed, ready to be picked up by her dad soon (though I suspected Sandie had told Mr Walker not to come and get her for ages yet, till she got a good gawp at my relatives).

"No – it was Billy."

"Yeah? How is he?" asked Kyra, sprawling her elbows over the surf-dude-and-pineapple tablecloth. "Still missing a brain cell or three?"

"Didn't know he had as many as three to begin with!" I grinned back at her, as me and Sandie did our little laundry dance. (*Fold! Step together, step apart, fold again...* It was like something that Dad would do at his line-dancing class.)

Kyra had ambled around to my house a quarter

of an hour ago, with the sole intention of reminding me, Sandie and any family members who happened to be listening that she was going on holiday tomorrow.

"There you go!" said Sandie, placing the newly washed, neatly folded duvet cover down on the kitchen table, right on top of a dollop of marmalade. And with a silent hop, Colin bounded up, clawing a purring circle of contentedness in the square of tumble-dried warm fabric.

"Thanks, Sand. Listen, Kyra, you don't *have* to hang around, you know. Shouldn't you be at home, packing?"

I was only winding her up. I knew she was way too nosey to miss out on the Canadians coming. And I was only getting her back for boasting about her week on the Costa de la Luz, and all the Spanish surfers she was hoping to ogle. She seemed to forget that just last week she'd been moaning about the sheer dreariness of being thirteen and hanging out with your parents in a strange place for a week, where your mobile doesn't even work.

"I'll just chuck a couple of bikinis in a bag," Kyra shrugged casually.

Yeah, *right*. The airline would be charging her mum and dad extra just to take Kyra's wardrobe-sized suitcase on board, I bet.

"They're *heeeerrrre*!"

Tor – our early warning system – had done his job well. He'd been on patrol out by the garden gate (with his trusty helpers, Rolf and Winslet) for the last twenty minutes, poised to run in and alert us (i.e., yell) as soon as he saw a car stuffed with relative strangers and Dad pull up outside.

I didn't even need to say, "Come on, then!" – my best friends were practically running ahead of me, nearly colliding with Linn, who was hastily stuffing the reluctant hoover in the cupboard under the stairs.

"Is this thing alive?" she muttered grumpily, as coils of tubing kept trying to escape and stop her from closing the door.

"Hurry up!" we all heard Rowan calling from the sunshiny front garden.

Rowan – wow, she'd really made an effort. Standing backlit by the sun in the doorway, she looked like an exotic cross between a maypole and Minnie Mouse: two high-set, backcombed, dark(er) brown bunches were bound up with a myriad of coloured ribbons, which dangled down in trails over her bare shoulders.

"Is that new?" I asked, glancing at her multi-coloured vest top, before staring at the faces staring back out at me from the people carrier that was just parking in a space a few metres up from our house.

"Tie-dyed it this morning, in-between airing the pillows."

I hoped for Rowan's sake her new vest was properly dried before she put it on. I knew she wanted to make an impression, but having multi-coloured skin might alarm rather than impress our guests. Don't know what they were going to make of the fake leopard tattoo on her arm either; but then at least it meant her heart'n'roses tattoo *had* been fake, since she'd washed that off and replaced it with this. Unless, of course, the *leopard* was the real thing...

"Wow! She looks *so* like your dad!" Sandie said enthusiastically, as an angular woman in shades stepped out of the car and waved at us.

"She's not actually related," Linn muttered behind us, a big, welcoming grin splashed across her face. "Our Uncle Joe is Dad's brother!"

"What, that big, fat guy?" asked Kyra, with her usual charm.

I don't know if it was just nerves, but the next couple of minutes felt like they were speeded up; like those time-lapse cameras they have on nature documentaries, showing flowers open their petals, and drop them at lightning speed. First, there was a bustle of car doors opening, and Dad, angular Auntie Pauline and, er, big, fat Uncle Joe poured out, followed by two serious-looking almost-identical small people (Carli and Charlie, unless my elf-radar was completely off-kilter) and a mountain of luggage.

And all of them – Dad, Uncle, Aunt, cousins and bags – came trundling at high, jumbled speed along the pavement towards the house and me, Linn, Ro, Tor, Sandie and Kyra, to a soundtrack of "hi!"s and excitable barking. And then there were random hugs and kisses and hellos and licks (the latter courtesy of an overexcited Rolf).

Then time started slowing down, and I got my first proper look at the newly rediscovered branch of my family. Uncle Joe: fatter (and balder) than the photos I'd seen of him, but then they were a decade or so out of date. But he seemed pretty smiley, which was good sign, I hoped. Auntie Pauline: skinnier (and more made-up) than the photos I'd seen of her, but she was ruffling Tor's hair affectionately, which I hoped was a good sign too. As for Carli and Charlie ... well, they looked *exactly* like they did in the photo we'd had last Christmas. The word "elf" came to mind...

But it wasn't just *us* doing the looking.

"Ooh, aren't you the spitting image of your

mum, Linnhe?" Auntie Pauline beamed at my oldest sister.

That was nice. That made me go slightly wibbly inside.

"And this little one!" Auntie Pauline continued, smiling down at my adorable brother. "Poor thing! How could any mother desert a darling boy like this?"

Um, that seemed less than tactful. But maybe the long journey had made my aunt say things she'd never come out with normally.

"Hey, I knew you and Melanie had loads of kids, but I didn't think it was *this* many!" chortled Uncle Joe, glancing around us all.

"Um, well, these are Ally's very good friends," Dad explained, pointing to my mates, "Sandie and Kyra!"

"Ha!" Uncle Joe beamed at my nodding, smiling friends. "That makes sense. Knew *that* one was kind of the wrong colour!"

That one – Kyra – stopped smiling instantly, as did me, Sandie and my entire family. Somehow, jet-lag wasn't really an excuse for that particularly clunky comment.

All of a sudden, I felt my pancake heart flip over into a belly-flop. It wasn't just what Uncle Joe and Auntie Pauline had said that filled me with dread; it was the fact that simultaneously, I'd just noticed…

a) my cousin Carli backing away from loveable, lickable Rolf like he had rabies;

b) my cousin Charlie staring at my groovily eccentric sister Rowan with a look of pure horror and contempt on his face;

c) my uncle blankly ignore a cat that wasn't Colin's purring welcome at his feet;

d) my aunt's pure, undisguised distaste as she caught sight of the (plastic) Hawaiian aloha flower garland Rowan had carefully draped around the "El Paradiso" sign above the front door.

"How funny!" said Auntie Pauline, studying the neighbouring fork windchimes without a trace of a smile on her face.

"Is business so bad you've got to open your house as a junk shop, Martin?" Uncle Joe chuckled loudly.

"Well, it's just—"

But before Dad got a chance to reply, we all became aware of a whining sob.

"What's wrong, darling?" Auntie Pauline dropped to her knees beside a wailing Charlie.

"He hates London. He wants to go home," Carli replied flatly.

It was spooky – while her nine-year-old brother

was doing an excellent impression of a tempera-mental toddler, Carli had the detached, bored look of a middle-aged woman (only in miniature).

"Listen, is it OK if I phone my dad and see if he's on his way?" Sandie whispered in my ear.

Great. If Sandie – the kindest girl in the world – was desperate to get out of here, the omens must be bad.

"Can I get a lift, Sandie?" Kyra asked bluntly, just as keen to make her escape.

And thanks to the knot of dread that had suddenly twisted itself up in my tummy, I was quite tempted to ask Sandie if there was space in her dad's car for me too…

Chapter 5

THOSE FIRST (BAD) IMPRESSIONS...

"*Grrrrrrrrrrr…!*"

That was my Uncle Joe, giving my dad his fortieth bear-hug since he and his family had arrived at ours.

"Got a lot of catching up to do, eh, bruv?"

Dad tried not to wince under the jokey punch my uncle had just landed on his arm, nearly making him drop the carton of juice he'd been trying to pour into the jug by the sink.

"Um, sure!" Dad nodded enthusiastically. "Have a seat and something to eat, Joe!"

"*Grrrrrrrrrrr…!*"

That wasn't Uncle Joe this time; that was Winslet.

Dodging past the considerable bulk of my uncle, I bent down and flipped the lock on the cat-flap so that Winslet couldn't stick her head through and growl at us any more.

I hated having to put her outside in the garden, but she needed to calm down for a bit. She'd been grumpy ever since Charlie had accidentally kicked her on the way into the house when he first arrived. Funnily enough, Rolf was keeping a pretty wide berth of my cousin too, even though Charlie was currently dropping plenty of crumbs on the floor, as he poured a mountain of Pringles on to his plate.

"Hey, Martin," said Uncle Joe, checking out the white plastic picnic seat he was settling himself into, "what's the deal with these? Got something against normal chairs?"

"Ha, ha!" Dad laughed self-consciously, as he plonked the big pitcher of orange juice in the middle of the kitchen table.

Parents: whether you like them loads or they drive you nuts, you have to admit that generally they seem to act like they're in control. But today, there was no *way* my dad was in control. In fact, he was so relieved when Grandma turned up ten minutes before that I thought he was going to *kiss* her (you should have seen how confused that made Grandma). The trouble was, I guess, that Dad is kind of shy around the edges, and though normally you don't tend to notice that too much, stand him next to our uncle and suddenly he came over a bit like a bumbly, nervous schoolkid in front of a booming, bombastic headteacher.

Anyway, Grandma immediately started taking

charge (as soon as she'd ducked away from Dad's unexpected kiss), cheerily saying her hellos to the new Loves and getting stuck into making up the snacks that me, Linn and Rowan had been too busy with laundry/stunned at the new arrivals to organize. She'd even ordered me and Rowan next door to beg a couple of plastic picnic chairs from our neighbours Michael The Vet and Harry, to supplement our ongoing chair crisis round the kitchen table.

"But pretend it's for the garden!" Grandma had warned us. "If they know it's for indoors, they'll only try and lend you a couple of their beautiful dining-room chairs, and I'm not having that!"

It wasn't as if Grandma had anything *against* beautiful dining-room chairs – in fact, I'm sure she'd *love* to see stuff like that in our kitchen instead of the mismatching set of wobbly old seats we use (and wobble on) every day. It's just that she was practical enough to know that it might harm future neighbourly relations if we handed Michael and Harry back two chairs that had been lightly scratched by cats, chewed by dogs, covered in a fine haze of mucky fingerprints and pet hair, and with the odd chunk missing from the legs thanks to Tor careering into them as his toy ambulance rushed various members of his Beany Babies collection to Rolf's Animal Hospital (the vegetable rack in the utility room).

"Well, this all very ... um ... *bohemian!*" Auntie Pauline proclaimed, drumming her fingers on the red-patterned tablecloth, and letting her eyes rest on the illuminated Croatia poster. "Wait till you see *our* house – we've brought photos – it's a dream! Detached and interior designed, of course, and it's right next to one of *the* best sports clubs with tennis courts and a golf course. And it's very close to the children's school which is one of *the* best in Toronto, and—"

"God, sausage rolls! Haven't had these in years!" Uncle Joe cheerfully interrupted, while helping himself to the plates of nibbles Grandma had set out. "Yuck – and now I remember why!"

It wasn't as if Grandma had slaved over a hot stove and made the food with her own fair hands today (someone at Tesco did that), but I seemed to remember that it wasn't polite to pull faces the minute you ate something you didn't like when you're a guest in someone else's house. And he hadn't even tasted Rowan's cooking yet. How rude was he going to be about that?

He wasn't the only one. Charlie and Carli had been ominously quiet in the hour since they'd arrived, and they were still quiet now, apart from the sound of Charlie spitting out part of a sandwich he'd just bitten into. Honestly, from the look on his face you'd think it was filled with earthworms and sludge instead of tuna mayonnaise.

"Oh, sweetie!" Auntie Pauline cooed at Charlie, as Carli looked impassively on. "Are you feeling a little sick? It must be the jet-lag!"

"It's this! It's *disgusting*! Can't we go to McDonald's?"

Auntie Pauline and Uncle Joe burst into gales of laughter as their little darling held up his pretty ordinary sandwich like it was an unexploded time bomb or something.

I did a quick face check of my family and saw that everyone was wearing the same slightly startled expression as me. Good grief, me and my sisters and brother might not go to *the* best schools, but at least we knew how to behave. What did they teach in Charlie's school, anyway? Lessons in international rudeness?

Staring is rude too, and that's exactly what Carli was doing right now, her beady, birdy dark eyes gazing unblinkingly in my direction. I tried an uncertain smile in her direction, but instead of smiling back, she simply transferred her stare on to Tor, who was sitting to one side of me and constructing a teetering tower out of kettle chips.

"Mummy…"

"What is it, Carli, darling?" asked Auntie Pauline, still recovering from her chuckles at Charlie.

"That little boy is playing with his food!"

"'That little boy'!" Auntie Pauline repeated with a giggle. "That little boy is your cousin Tor, sweetie!"

"Why does he have such a silly name?"

That sent Uncle Joe and Auntie Pauline off into hysterics again.

"Honestly, the things kids say!" Uncle Joe managed to splutter through his chuckles.

"I was just trying to build the CN Tower…" Tor muttered, knocking aside his kettle-chip sculpture and looking truly hurt.

He'd shown me and Linn a picture of Toronto's CN Tower this morning, when we were hanging pillowcases on the line and trying to stop Rolf eating all the clothes pegs. The tower was in a book he had about world records; he stood and carefully read aloud some blurb about it being the world's tallest free-standing building or something while we pretended to be interested. Poor Tor – with that one page he'd done more background research into our visitors than the rest of us put together, and here they were, dissing his efforts and telling him his name was silly.

And anyway, who was Carli to talk about silly names? I mean, hers was practically identical to her twin brother's (minus the odd vowel and consonant).

"Well, Carli," my dad managed a taut smile across the table, "it's not *really* a silly name. Tor is named after a very historic place in England called Glastonbury Tor, and the word Tor itself means—"

"It means Melanie always did have an over-active imagination when it came to naming her kids!" chortled Uncle Joe.

Being a) on our best behaviour, and b) too taken aback to know what to say or do, Linn and Rowan stayed as silent and stunned as I was. Grandma was on her best behaviour too, but she wasn't about to stay silent when people were potentially criticizing her daughter or grandkids.

"Well, I think Melanie and Martin put a lot of thought into naming each of the children," she announced tersely, meaning, I was sure, that Uncle Joe and Auntie Pauline obviously hadn't. ("Hey, what rhymes with Charlie? Carli! Yeah, *that'll* do!")

"So when's Melanie going to put some thought into coming back home to you guys, then?" Uncle Joe grinned broadly.

I decided at that precise moment that my uncle

was a marvel to the modern medical world, born as he was without a shred of tact in his body. Dad looked white as one of the white pillowcases still dancing out on the line behind him in the garden.

"Listen!" said Grandma, clapping her hands together and gazing around at the rest of us, completely ignoring Uncle Joe and his comment. "Ally, why don't you and Tor take Carli and Charlie and their bags up to your rooms and get them settled in?"

Nice bit of diverting from Grandma, there.

"Coming?" I tried smiling at our unsmiling cousins, leading the way, along with Tor, towards the hall, the bags and the stairs.

As I left the kitchen, I heard two things: Grandma saying, "Well, what about showing us these photos of your house?" and a muffled loud growl coming from the vicinity of the cat-flap...

"And that's Alexandra Palace way over there," I explained, pointing proudly at the amazing view from my bedroom window. "Only people call it Ally Pally for short. And Dad calls me that too, since I was named after—"

"It's very small."

I whipped my head round and realized that my cousin Carli was paying not the slightest bit of attention to me or my mini-history of Crouch End. Instead, she was gazing around my blue attic bedroom with its big, old map of the word and cloud-covered duvet and hanging, blow-up globe and wishing – I could tell – that she wasn't there. Much like I was, to be honest.

"It's *cosy*," I replied, putting a giant dollop of emphasis on the last word.

"It's not as nice as that room across the hall."

"Linn's?"

"Yeah, her. Your dad says she's not going to be staying here."

You know, it was hard to believe Carli was only a couple of years older than Tor; the way she blinked her dark, little eyes slowly and confidently at me, you'd think she'd swallowed a superiority pill.

"Um, that's right. Linn's going to be sleeping over at my gran's flat."

"So, can't I sleep in *her* room?"

"*No*," I said, trying to stop myself from sounding bugged by her pushiness. "My dad's going to have that room, and your parents are going to get his room!"

As Carli tutted and rolled her eyes, I bit my lip and turned to open a drawer. (Don't worry – I wasn't about to stuff her into it, although that was tempting. I was only planning on emptying it to give her some space to unpack.)

"So, what are you looking forward to seeing in London?" I tried to chatter brightly while slamming my socks into the second drawer down. "Madame Tussaud's is pretty good, specially the ride at the—"

"*Aaaaaaaaaaaaaaaaaaghhhhhhhhhhhhhhhhhh!*"

For quite a small person, Carli sure could scream loud…

MONDAY MORNING MOANING

"Ro!" I whispered.

My sister's hair wobbled across the pillow as I tried to shake her awake, looking darker than ever across the white cotton. Speaking of white cotton, I noticed there was a yellow, spotty hind leg on the sheet, close to Ro's shoulder. Looked like the leopard (another fake – phew) had started peeling off in the night.

"What's up?" Ro yawned herself awake, her arms stretching so wide I nearly got a punch on the nose.

"Got a proposition for you."

Rowan wriggled into a sitting position and eyeballed me. "Oh, yeah? What kind of a proposition?"

"Let Carli sleep in here with you, and I'll buy you a new set of fairy lights!"

"Ally, much as I'd love another set of fairy lights, I've got so many in here already Dad says I'll make the fusebox explode!"

"Well, if you let Carli stay here with you, then…"

I was struggling: I'd been positive that the lure of fairy lights would be a sure-fire hit.

"...then I'd be an idiot," Rowan finished my sentence in her own way. "No *way* is she coming in here!"

"Ro!" I squeaked at her lack of sisterly support.

"Oh, poor Ally – is it horrible?" she asked, as if she could read my frazzled mind.

Of course it was horrible. I now had to share a room with someone who a) was a neurotic scream-ing freak (I mean, who could get upset by Colin, just lying there in the corner of my room?), b) called the nicest cat in the world "gross", all because he has the misfortune of having only three legs, and c) got the pets banned from my room for the duration of her stay, 'cause – as Auntie Pauline put it – she can't have her little girl "waking up in the night being traumatized by animals".

Uh, excuse me – don't they have grizzly bears and wolves in Canada? Probably not in the shopping malls that Carli seemed to spend ninety per cent of her time in, and which I'd had to hear her going on and *on* about last night while I was trying to go to sleep. And even once Carli finally stopped bragging about all the clothes her mum bought her in the malls and nodded off herself, I stayed firmly awake, listening to the endless scratching at the door and irate cat "prrps!" and dog snuffles from my locked-out furry buddies.

I knew Uncle Joe and his family had only been in our lives a few hours and that maybe I should give them more of a chance to grow on me, but right now, I was ratty through lack of sleep and in the mood to moan. And if you can't moan to your mad, middle sister, then who *can* you moan to...?

"Ro – I don't want to spend the day alone with them," I mumbled, lifting up a hunk of duvet and curling up under it at the other end of the bed for comfort.

By alone, I meant me, Rowan and Tor, who'd found ourselves invited along as tour guides on The Other Loves' first day out in London. Linn and Dad wriggled out of joining us with the excuse that they were working (OK, they didn't exactly wriggle and they were genuinely working), and as Grandma wasn't directly related to them, she was excused. (Lucky Grandma...)

"It's only for one day! Dad's got that guy covering for him at the shop tomorrow so he'll be coming with us, then!"

I don't know why Rowan was being so positive; last night Auntie Pauline had beamed at her and said, "Your sister Linnhe is *such* a pretty girl. And you could be too!" Talk about a back-handed, face-slapping compliment. Still, at least she thought Linn and Ro were somewhere in the *spectrum* of pretty; she hadn't said anything to me about my appearance, which meant she probably thought I took after my dad, i.e. looked like a man.

Eeeeekkkk!

We both spun around as Rowan's bedroom door suddenly creaked open, and in slinked Tor, shutting the door behind him and padding over at high speed for the bed, where Rowan had the duvet held up ready for him to join us.

"Is Charlie still asleep?" I asked him.

Tor nodded, while tenderly stroking the pocket in his Spiderman pyjama top.

"Who've you got in there?" Rowan frowned.

"Beckham," Tor replied, fishing out a small white mouse and letting it sniff around in the cupped palms of his hands. "He's upset."

"Why's he upset?"

Seemed to me like *Tor* was the one who was upset. His dark eyebrows were furrowed together to make one long caterpillar of hair on his forehead.

"Charlie."

Uh-oh.

"What did Charlie do?" Rowan prompted our little brother.

"Spun the mouse wheel really fast when Beckham was in it, then laughed when Beckham fell out."

Well, taunting innocent wheel-trotting mice wasn't exactly a great way to become best mates with my brother. But it wasn't just the 1000 kilometre an hour free-fall whirling that had got Charlie in Tor's bad books. Poking sticks at the hamsters was bad too, specially when those sticks turn out to be Tor's much-beloved stick *insects*.

"I'm sure Charlie didn't mean it," said Ro, stroking Beckham with her finger. "He was probably just a bit overexcited at seeing all the animals in your room."

Tor and I exchanged looks that said, "Yeah, *that'll* be right."

"Come on, you two – give him a chance! *And* the rest of them! They had a long flight; they were probably just tired. I bet they'll be totally different today!"

Oh, *I* got it. In the absence of Linn, Rowan was taking on board the responsible, eldest-in-the-family role.

"And remember, we've got to make an effort for Dad's sake," she continued. "After all, apart from us, Uncle Joe *is* his only relation!"

OK, she had a point. OK, she'd made me feel

guilty. Dad did trust us to make an effort and I didn't want to let him down. So for Dad's sake, I'd try to like Carli, and the important thing to remember was that I only had to try and like her for two weeks.

"Maybe Charlie isn't so bad..." Tor mumbled, giving a little shrug, Ro's mini-speech obviously giving him a dose of guilt too.

"That's right, Tor! I bet he's really sorry for—*oh*."

Rowan's unexpected "oh" caught our attention. And the reason for it? One dog of the Rolf variety, slinking unhappily into the room wearing a white sports sock on each of his four paws, held in place with rubber bands.

Wonder how that could have happened...?

Chapter 7

MINE'S BETTER THAN *YOURS*...

You know how Hindus have a different kind of Christmas-type thing, called Diwali? Well, I first heard about it in primary school, when the teacher asked Nisha Patel to get up and give us a talk about that, and her visit to her grandparents' village in Gujarat.

I don't remember too much about what Nisha said exactly – apart from the fact that she hated the outside toilet but loved all the home-made sweets her relatives forced her to eat. But I *do* remember that I was fascinated to hear all about another country.

Same goes for Kellie's mum, who's told us loads of funny stories about being a little girl growing up in Jamaica, and Chloe always comes back with tonnes of tales from Ireland when she goes to stay with her nan.

The point is, some people can make a place sound *so* interesting you could listen to them yak on about it all day. But then you get other people who just *boast* about where they're from till you want to shove a travel guide down their neck to shut them up.

"Daddy, I like the CN Tower better, 'cause you can see all of Toronto!"

An old couple standing near us in the pod started smirking when Carli said that, and no wonder. We were up at the very top of the revolving London Eye, with historic stuff like Big Ben and the Thames and St Paul's Cathedral dotted down below, not to mention the whole of London itself, sprawling all the way to the horizon, practically. And what did Carli want to see? Toronto. London wasn't good enough, as you could tell from the way she was standing leaning against the glass, with her back to the view.

"It's not as good as the CN Tower, is it, Daddy?"

"Well, this is just a big, old bicycle wheel, isn't it?" Uncle Joe guffawed. "Is that why you wanted us to come on this thing, Martin?"

"Um, no..." Dad shook his head. "I just think it's an amazing piece of structural engineering and thought it would be a great experience for the kids."

"Hey, lighten up! Take a joke!"

Uncle Joe did another of his jovial thumps on Dad's back. Dad was going to be black and blue at this rate, and it was only Day Three of the visit from the Relatives From Hell.

Tor tugged at my sleeve and I bent down to let him whisper in my ear.

"If he does that again to Dad, I'm going to kick him!"

"Don't do that," I whispered back hurriedly. "Dad doesn't mind. Honest!"

It was hard to tell if Dad did or didn't – the house had been so crowded with people and talking and bustle the last couple of days that it was impossible to work out *what* was going on with him. But from the way he was frowning over Uncle Joe's shoulder, I think he might have noticed Carli's snidey remarks and Charlie's pet-teasing antics over the last few days – he was probably being just too polite to say anything about it out loud.

And at least he was here with me and Tor today. Yesterday was torture: we took an open-top bus tour of London which Carli and Charlie yawned and complained through, while Uncle Joe and Auntie Pauline spent all their time talking about how much London had gone downhill since they'd left. Apart from that, me, Tor and Rowan had heard (endlessly) about the modern Toronto City Hall ("so much more stunning than the Houses of Parliament!"), the SkyDome ("The whole roof comes off! Bet you have nothing like that here!"), Toronto shops ("So much better than London's!"), Toronto parks ("So much cleaner than London's!"), and even Toronto squirrels ("They're black! So much more unusual than the grey ones here!").

By the end of the day, I wondered why my uncle and aunt hadn't just stayed at home and gawped at the wonders of Toronto and saved themselves a few hundred dollars in airfares.

And so much for Rowan being the voice of reason yesterday morning; after a whole day of the Relatives From Hell wittering on – especially the fashion and grooming tips Auntie Pauline liked to drop into the conversation when she was talking to Ro – my sister had had enough. That's why today she was skiving; sorry, I mean too "ill" to come out with us.

Funny how I saw her helping herself to three Hob-nobs from the biscuit tin when she claimed to have a dodgy tummy...

"Ally..."

Tor was tugging at my sleeve again.

"What is it?" I asked, bending down to listen to more whispers.

"Look at what Charlie's doing!"

Tor was pretty wary of Charlie, specially after the way he'd spectacularly denied having anything to do with the Rolf-in-Socks incident. When Rowan tried to tactfully bring up the matter at breakfast yesterday, Charlie had burst into tears and run sobbing to his mum. We might have been taken in if it wasn't for the fact that Rolf tried (and failed) to squash himself through the cat-flap in a panic as soon as he wandered into the kitchen and set eyes on Charlie.

And right now, our lovely cousin was breathing steamy circles on the window and writing swear words in them.

Part of me wondered if I should point out their darling son's handiwork to Uncle Joe and Auntie Pauline, but for one thing, the evidence would probably melt away the minute they turned to check it out; for another, I'm not a telltale.

"Just ignore him, he's being a horrible boy," I hissed at Tor, before straightening up.

"Mummy..."

That was Carli, just about to tell her mum that Big Ben was boring or that Buckingham Palace looked like a dump or something.

"What is it, sweetie?"

"Ally and Tor keep whispering all the time..."

Well, *I* might not be a telltale, but it looked liked Carli certainly was.

* * *

"Hi!" trilled Rowan, smiling up at us all as we trudged into the kitchen after our thrilling day out, criticizing every tourist attraction London has to offer.

For someone who was supposed to be ill (ha!), Rowan was looking very healthy. She'd even managed to crimp her hair – and dye it another shade darker, if I wasn't very much mistaken.

"Feeling better, Rowan?" asked Dad, at the kitchen doorway.

"Much!" she nodded enthusiastically.

She'd *better* be better – better enough to rejoin Tor and me on our travels with the Relatives From Hell tomorrow...

"What's this, then?"

Auntie Pauline noseyed at a pile of photos Rowan had in her hands.

"Oh, they're snaps from the barbecue we went to next door a couple of weeks ago," Rowan explained. "Our neighbours just dropped them round for us to have a look at."

"Lovely couple," Dad chipped in. "That's them there..."

It was fascinating to watch Auntie Pauline and Uncle Joe's stunned reaction when Dad took a photo from Rowan and passed it over for them to see: they obviously hadn't expected the lovely couple to be two *blokes*.

"Look, this one's cute!" said Rowan, passing on another picture to my speechless aunt and uncle. "Do you remember that, Ally? When that ladybird landed on my arm and Tor got in a panic that I'd hurt it?"

"Yeah, I remember," I nodded, leaning over and inspecting the shot of me, Rowan, the tiny red dot on her arm and Tor doing his Dr Doolittle impression – trying to talk the insect into stepping on his finger so he could remove it to safety.

"Call that an insect?" Uncle Joe blustered, getting his composure back. "You should *see* the size of some of the dragonflies in the woods back in Toronto!"

"Ro..." Tor's voice interrupted from over by the sink.

He was staring at a cardboard box, which appeared to be shedding straw and moving slightly.

"Oh, I forgot!" Rowan burst out. "Michael dropped that off for you, Tor. One of his clients has had to go into hospital for a couple of weeks, and he thought you'd be the perfect person to look after this man's tortoise while he's away."

"Brilliant! Eh, Tor?" said Dad, picking the box up and gently lowering it down for Tor – and Carli and Charlie – to peek inside.

Tor was so chuffed he looked like he was ready to self-combust. From Carli and Charlie's expressions, they've might as well have been gawping at a dog poo in a shell.

"Oh, and another thing!" said Rowan, a little too brightly for someone sick. "I've got a summer job!"

"Since when!" I blurted out.

"Since today! I was just passing ... I mean, *Von* was just passing a hairdresser's near Camden Market and they had a notice in the window. So I went in ... um, I *phoned* up, and I got it, just like that!"

"A hairdresser, eh? That's nice! Maybe they can give your hair a bit of a tidy up..." muttered Auntie Pauline, eyeing up Rowan's uneven layers of crimping.

Was she kidding? Had she *seen* the shops in Camden Market? Rowan was more likely to come back with a pink mohican and dreadlocks than a nice, neat bob.

"Well done, Ro!" said Dad proudly, patting her on the shoulder. "So, are you going to be a junior? Washing hair and that sort of stuff?"

(Dad's great: he's not a pushy, ambitious parent at all. He'd be proud of *anything* we do, as long as it's not stuff like kicking in the glass in bus shelters or mugging old ladies.)

"Kind of. Probably more sweeping the floor and making cups of tea, I think!" Rowan beamed.

"And when do you start, exactly?" I narrowed my eyes at her, suddenly getting suspicious.

"Um, tomorrow!" Rowan said hurriedly, her cheeks turning pink under my accusing stare.

Great: I was being deserted by *everyone*. Feargal hadn't phoned, Billy wasn't interested in coming near me while I was contaminated with relations, Sandie hadn't returned the call I'd left last night on her answerphone, Kyra was off chatting up Spanish surf-dudes, Linn had moved out to Grandma's and now Rowan had gone and conveniently got herself a job to keep herself unavailable too.

Erm, she really *had* got a job, hadn't she? What with the fake tattoos, pretend illnesses and non-fake hair dye that she told Grandma she *wasn't* using, it was pretty hard to work out what exactly was going on with Ro at the moment...

Chapter 8

A LAZY DAY AND A BIG, FAT FIB

Rowan's white lies were catching.

Not that she'd been lying about having a job – that turned out to be true. "I'm really sorry, Ally!" she'd whispered to me at one point last night. "It'll do my *head* in to stay around these people! I just thought if I was working, it'd get me out of here, so I spent the whole day today looking for anything, anywhere!"

And so Rowan left bright and early this morning, all dressed up in her bangles and beads with big, felt flowers newly sewn on her old denim skirt and matching felt flowers glued on to her hairslides. She'd even left the name and phone number of the shop on a Post-It note beside the phone in case of emergencies. (What sort of emergencies? In case one of us needed an urgent trim or something?)

No – it was her lie about the dodgy tummy that was catching...

"They are *freaky*!" Billy had hissed at me up in my room last night, after curiosity had got the better of him and he'd cycled around to see me.

He'd been less than impressed with his first sightings of my cousins: Carli was having a tearful strop because the pizza Dad had ordered in had (omigod! Call the police!) green pepper on it, and Charlie was making what looked suspiciously like a noose with the lace out of one of his trainers.

"Tell me about it!" I'd replied, noticing a splodge of mauve nail varnish on top of the table that hadn't been there before. Had Carli been mucking around with my stuff?

"Your uncle's so loud! And his joke's are *so* not funny!"

Too right. I mean, what was amusing about calling Billy my "boyfriend" fifteen thousand times in a row, when he'd only been in the house five minutes? And Billy really didn't appreciate the grilling he'd got about his fashion sense (i.e. his fraying long skate shorts) from Auntie Pauline either.

"I can't stand the thought of hanging around with them for a whole day again tomorrow!" I'd sighed.

"Well, can't you say something to your dad?"

"God, no! He really wants us all to get along, and he hasn't seen Uncle Joe in nearly ten years – it could be another ten years before he sees him again!"

"Be sick, then."

"What?" I'd frowned at Billy. Sometimes it's very hard to understand the workings of his mind.

"Catch whatever Rowan was pretending to have!" he grinned at me.

I was all ready to protest, when I realized I just couldn't face another day of the Relatives From Hell moaning and complaining. All I had to do was persuade Tor to join in the lie (I hated to do it, but I could hardly let him suffer on his own).

"Isn't he cute?" I heard Tor's voice ask now, as an ET lookalike suddenly appeared in front of my face, all wrinkles and trusting eyes.

"He's a lovely tortoise," I agreed, backing away from it slightly, in case Spartacus (the tortoise) thought my fringe was an interesting piece of vegetation at such close quarters.

Oh, yes – me and Tor had been having a lovely day all to ourselves in the house. Well, at least Tor had; spending hours and hours blissfully tending his brood of furry, scaly beasts. Me, I'd been too wrapped up in guilt (at fibbing to Dad about the sore stomachs, mine and Tor's) and boredom. OK, so I didn't want to hang out with my relatives, but I wouldn't have minded the odd friend popping round to say hello while I babysat Tor. But no one – not Sandie, not Chloe or the others – had phoned me back after the messages I'd left them the last couple of days. And I'm not even going to mention who else hadn't called...

All right, I will, then. It was Wednesday, i.e. it had been exactly ten days since my not-quite-date with Feargal. What had I done so wrong that Feargal hadn't bothered phoning me back for another not-quite-date? Maybe it was the fact that once we'd talked about the people we both knew (Kyra etc.) the conversation ground to a halt. Or maybe it was the fact that his greatest love in the world is hip-hop, which I know nothing about, apart from a couple of songs that have been in the charts. (When I mentioned them, he burst out laughing, like I'd said I was into the Tweenies or something.) And then when we were saying good-bye, I think he *may* have been planning on kissing me, but when he leant forward I panicked, mumbled something about having a stone in my shoe and bent down so fast I think I cracked his front tooth with my head.

Hmm ... maybe *that's* why he hadn't phoned me; he'd been getting extensive dental work done after my assault on him...

Oops. And here came something spooky: just as I was dodging Spartacus the tortoise and thinking about Feargal (not that they look alike, honest), the phone rang.

"Hello?" I muttered into the receiver, as a set of keys rattled in the front door and The Other Loves arrived home from what was bound to have been a disastrous day out at the Tower of London.

I waved at the weary faces of my aunt and uncle and at the miserable gobs of my twin cousins, who were both looking particularly surreal today. Miserable cousin number one (Charlie) had a spangly pair of deely-boppers on his head while miserable cousin number two (Carli) was wearing a bowler hat with *I* ❤ *London* on it. Had the shop run out of *I hate London* logos, then?

"Ally?"

"Yes?" I nodded, dragging my attention back to the call.

"It's Feargal."

You'd think my heart was fixed to a rubber band, the way it *boing*ed around my chest.

"Um, hi, Feargal," I grinned like a big dope, as my Relatives From Hell hung up their coats, dumped their bags and scattered themselves through the house.

"Listen … fancy meeting up again?"

I actually fancied knowing what had taken him so long to phone me, but then Kyra and Salma told me that's just what boys do, so I just left that thought to drift…

"Er … yeah. That would be nice."

Nice. Boys hate the word "nice". Why couldn't I have picked a better word?

"What about tomorrow?"

Tomorrow was fine. I knew this because tomorrow, my Relatives From Hell were going to Guildford to visit Auntie Pauline's relations, so I didn't even need to fake a bad stomach.

"OK."

"Great. Want to meet in Priory Park again?"

"OK."

"About two o'clock?"

"OK."

Good grief. Say something *apart* from "nice" and "OK", Ally…

"See you then!"

"OK, that'd be nice."

Aaarghh!

I had just put the phone down and was contemplating the fact that I was a complete moron, when my flapping ears caught a snatch of conversation coming from the living room.

"Don't know how her father can rest, a girl of that age having so many boyfriends!" I heard Auntie Pauline mutter. "I mean, letting her take that boy up to her room last night!"

Billy? Billy had been coming up to my room

since we were practically just able to crawl, never mind *walk* up the stairs. And what business was it of hers if I was talking to Feargal just now? It wasn't as if she was my—

"That girl really needs a mother! They *all* do!"

"Don't know if that would make any difference, Pauline," my uncle chuckled. "Melanie was never exactly a great influence, the way she dressed up like a hippy and acted so arty!"

I was so angry, I felt like screaming. Only someone started screaming first, and this time it wasn't Carli.

I flipped round and looked in the direction of the kitchen and the howl, but all I saw was Colin, sitting in the doorway with a pair of deely-boppers on his head, trying frantically to paw them off.

That didn't give me any clues as to what terrible thing had befallen cousin Charlie behind that closed door…

Chapter 9

THANK YOU, CARLI, THANK YOU *VERY* MUCH...

When Feargal asked me out, I think he kind of had the idea that this second not-quite-date would consist of just me and him – not me, him, two stupid, barky dogs and an unwelcome cousin.

Carli wasn't too thrilled at the dogs coming with us, but then I wasn't too thrilled at having to take Carli along either. And the reason I'd had to take them *all* on my not-quite-second-date was because of the terrible injuries Winslet had inflicted on my cousin Charlie the night before.

"My God, this place is a madhouse!" Auntie Pauline had shrieked, as she tried to comfort Charlie after his vicious savaging. "That dog ought to be put down! You can't keep your animals *or* your children under control!"

Dad, who'd ambled happily home from work to find sheer mayhem going on behind the front door, went slightly purple when she said that.

"For God's sake, Pauline! What are you talking about? The dog only gave his hand a little nip! She didn't even break the skin!"

"And she wouldn't have done it if Charlie hadn't tried to stuff her in the tumble dryer!" I'd butted in, as prime witness for the defence in the case of Winslet versus Charlie Love.

Poor Winslet; when I'd burst into the kitchen the night before, she'd been vainly trying to scrabble her way out of Charlie's arms (and vice-like grip), while Charlie was pointing her nose-first towards the ominous open door of the tumble dryer.

"I only wanted to see if she'd fit, Mummy!" Charlie sobbed theatrically, nestling his horrible little head on my aunt's chest. "I was only playing!"

"Of *course* you were, darling, of *course* you were," Auntie Pauline muttered, stroking his head. "Carli – has your father brought the car up to the door yet?"

"Pauline," Dad exclaimed, "there's really *no* need—"

"Martin – are you going to give us directions to the hospital or not?"

Dad did more than that; I guess he felt obliged to go with them to the casualty department. They were gone so long that me, Rowan, Linn, Tor and Carli had our tea without them. I filled Linn and Rowan in on the events but didn't make too much of an issue of it – not while Tor was sitting on the brink of tears with worry about what was going to happen to Winslet, and not while Carli was sitting staring malevolently at us all. (Wonder if she knew we were all brooding over how Charlie would like it if we tried stuffing *him* in the tumble dryer?)

Linn suggested that maybe Winslet should come back with her and stay at Grandma's for a while, but I pointed out that it wasn't a great idea – Winnie and Grandma's Siamese kitten Mushu don't really get along, and I didn't suppose our gran would appreciate the two of them playing hiss-chase around her neat flat.

Luckily, by the time the hospital party sloped back home, they seemed a lot calmer – apparently the doctor had very patiently explained that Charlie didn't have rabies or need plastic surgery, that all he might have was a tiny bruise, and that it really wasn't a good idea to try and "fit" dogs into tumble dryers. In fact, he'd really told Charlie off, which made Auntie Pauline furious – she called him a "very rude person". (Hey, it takes one to know one.) Still at least she and Uncle Joe had eased off on their demands to have Winslet put down now, even if they weren't very keen on seeing her around.

"Ally, I really think Charlie needs peace and quiet to recover today," Auntie Pauline had told me earlier, once she'd phoned her relations to postpone her family visit and settled Charlie on the sofa with a blanket and a mound of medicinal sweets and crisps. "Can you take Carli out with you this afternoon? And take those ... *animals* with you too, please?"

Grandma had popped round an hour before, and taken Tor out for the day (alerted by Linn last night, I think). Why hadn't Auntie Pauline asked *her* to take Carli along with *them*? Why was *I* stuck with her? Maybe because the only kind of luck I had was bad...

"Hi!" I said, way too loud.

Feargal, hunched up on the park bench with his headphones bulging out from his hood, didn't respond. (At least I *hoped* that's what they were, otherwise Feargal had grown some mean alien ears and also turned deaf since the last time I saw him.)

"Feargal!" I said louder, waving a hand in front of his face.

"Hey!" he grinned, sliding his headphones (phew!) off without disturbing his hood in any way. (A very skilful manoeuvre.)

He grinned a little less convincingly when he realized the girl and the dogs were with me, and not just strolling by.

"Um, Feargal, this is my cousin Carli."

"I'm from Canada."

"Uh-huh," nodded Feargal, eyeing Carli warily.

"She and her family are staying with us. And these are my dogs. The big dopey one is Rolf –"

Hearing his name, Rolf barked loudly, cocked his leg and widdled endearingly against the bench.

"– and the short, hairy one," I continued, pretending I hadn't just seen that, "is Winslet."

Winslet stopped chewing the empty Cornetto wrapper she'd picked up somewhere along the way and growled softly at Feargal, as if she was daring him to take it off her. Yeah, like he was really *desperate* for it.

"That dog's dangerous. It bit my brother."

"Yeah?"

Feargal frowned at Carli, at Winslet, and then at me.

"It wasn't a proper bite. Um ... do you want to walk?"

With a shrug, Feargal stood up and we began ambling along the path together, trailed by Carli, Rolf and Winslet (the girl and the dogs keeping a wide berth of each other).

"So, what were you listening to?" I tried to kick-start the conversation, aware that not-quite-date nerves were starting to strangle my throat, making my voice go squealy high-pitched.

"Public Enemy," said Feargal, flipping his CD

player open and rummaging around in his baggy trouser pocket for the sleeve.

I wished he'd take his hood down. It's the same as trying to have a conversation with someone wearing dark sunglasses; it's really disconcerting when you can't see a person's eyes or face properly (and Feargal had a very nice face that didn't deserve to be hidden away).

"Here…"

Oh. He was handing me the CD.

"It's old, but I thought you might … y'know, I thought I'd lend it to you since you don't know much about hip-hop."

"*Fear of a Black Planet…*" I read the album name out loud, hoping I wasn't as pink as I felt (fat chance).

"Yeah, it's an import copy my cousin got from America when it first came out," he said proudly.

I hadn't a clue why that might be important, and I hadn't heard of Public Enemy or their album, but I was very, very touched. It made this feel almost like a real date, if it wasn't for—

"Look! I know what *that* means!" spluttered an excitable voice, as Carli sidled in between us both and stabbed a pointy finger at a sticker on the front of the album. "'Advisory'! That means there's bad words on that album!"

"What – bad words like your brother was writing on the window when we were on the London Eye?" I blurted out.

Oops. How did that slip out?

Carli fixed an evil stare at me, then slunk back behind us. She couldn't argue with that – she'd probably seen what Charlie was up to as clearly as Tor and I had.

I glanced back at Feargal, and saw him meet my eyes – I tried to flash him the cute smile I knew he liked (he wrote that down in the journal he temporarily stole from me), but he looked away just before I dazzled him with it.

And then there was a long, long, *long* silence (apart from dog panting). For a millisecond, I thought about asking Feargal how his front teeth were after me bashing them last time we met, but that seemed too excruciatingly embarrassing a subject to bring up.

"Uh ... so how's your ankle?" Feargal finally spoke into the void.

"It's better. I mean, not *totally* better. I don't need the crutch any more but I've still got to wear a brace thing all the time. Well, not *all* the time – I can take it off in the bath. And ... um ... in bed."

Damn, damn, damn... I was not only blabbering endlessly, but I'd just gone bright pink again, blushing like a prim Victorian lady at the very idea of me mentioning "bath" and "bed" in front of a member of the opposite "sex". Omigod, I'd just thought the word "sex" and gone from pink to scarlet...

"*Ally* had a *boy* in her bedroom the other night for nearly an *hour*..."

Somehow without me noticing, Carli had slunk in between us again.

"Don't be silly, Carli! That was just my mate Billy!" I tried to laugh, but I could feel Feargal's eyes boring into me.

"My mummy said it's not right to have so many boyfriends at your age."

It might not be right to murder your cousin at my age, but if Carli carried on the way she was going, I'd be locked up in Holloway Prison by the end of the week.

"I don't *have* any boyfriends, Carli!" I turned round and hissed at her. "Billy is just a friend, and ... and..."

I couldn't finish that sentence 'cause I wasn't sure what Feargal *was* exactly yet. And even if Feargal *did* turn out to be my boyfriend (blush, blush), it wasn't any of Carli or her know-it-all mother's business.

"Billy?" Feargal suddenly blurted out. "Is that the geezer from Kyra's party?"

"Yeah! You remember Billy, don't you? Nice guy, bit of an idiot…"

That wasn't a great way to talk about Billy to someone I didn't know very well, but it was a short-cut way of trying to let Feargal know that Billy was nothing but a buddy.

"He's just a mate?" Feargal eyeballed me.

"He's just a mate!"

"For sure?"

"For sure!"

This was weird. How dare Feargal go all possessive on me, when we weren't even going out properly? I mean, wasn't I allowed to have a boy buddy? I wouldn't mind if he had girl mates… Except he didn't, did he? He only ever hung around with his posse of Baz, the two Mikeys and Ishmail.

"When *I* came in the bedroom to get my hairbrush, you and Billy were *lying* on the bed!"

"We were *sitting* on the bed!" I darted my eyes angrily at Carli.

Excuse me if I don't have a room big enough to fit a three-seater sofa in. Excuse me if the only comfy place to sit in my room is the bed, once your bum's gone numb from lounging on the floor…

Feargal seemed to be staring at the ground – you

could tell by the angle of his hood. Something told me he wasn't pleased.

"We were sitting on the bed!" I repeated, but this time directly to Feargal and in a much softer, more pleading voice.

"When I told my mummy that you were lying on the bed she said it was all your mummy's fault for being a bad influence. She said—"

"Carli!" I frowned down at her. "Will you shut up for five seconds? And don't you dare say stuff like that about my mum!"

"But my mummy says—"

"Uh ... listen," Feargal interrupted the row that was brewing between me and my obnoxious, telltale of a cousin (who couldn't even tell a tale without getting it way, way, *way* wrong). "I think I'd better head. Got ... y'know ... stuff."

My muddy brown eyes met his velvety brown eyes and in a split second I knew I'd been chucked, which was a crushing blow since I'd never properly known we were going out till now.

"Can I have my CD back? It's just that my cousin might not like it if I lend it out, since it's an import and everything..."

"Sure," I said, handing it over and hoping my hand didn't look as shaky as it felt (fat chance again).

"See you then," Feargal shrugged, and mooched

off towards the nearest park exit, with Rolf – doughball that he was – barking and loping after him.

"Where's he going?" Carli stared sullenly up at me.

I looked away from her, counting to ten. OK, so things hadn't exactly sparkled into life between me and Feargal on either of our dates, and I definitely didn't want to go out with someone who was so possessive and took the word of a gossiping nine-year-old stranger over me. But I'd have liked to find out his faults in my own time, not have Little Miss Telltale do it for me.

"Where are we going?" I heard Carli ask, as I stomped off down the path in the direction of the main gate.

"Home," I muttered over my shoulder. "Rolf! Here, boy!"

And wonky ankle or not, me, Winslet and Rolf were going to walk home really, *really* fast, so that Carli didn't have enough *breath* to talk to me. One more word from her today and I might scream.

"When we get back…" I suddenly heard her puffing to keep up behind me, "I'm going to tell Mummy that *you* were going to listen to a bad record with rude, bad swear words!"

It was just as well a woman was pushing her little

kid past us just then, or I might have been tempted to shout a very rude, bad swear word right at Carli...

Chapter 10

TIME OFF FOR GOOD BEHAVIOUR

"Ally? It's Chloe."

Hallelujah! My friends hadn't been abducted by aliens! They were alive! Well, at least one of them was, and that was better than nothing.

"I phoned you days ago, Chloe. Where've you been?" I asked her, a smile splitting my face, I was so glad to hear a friendly voice. It was now Friday, Day 6 of the living hell that was my life (felt like Day 600, actually), and after nearly a week's worth of pain-in-the-neck relatives and a little light dumping courtesy of Feargal O'Leary, I deserved a break.

(Oh, and speaking of relatives, one was hanging over the bannister right now, staring intently at me and listening in to my phone conversation.)

"I've just been doing stuff. You know how it is in the holidays!" Chloe said casually.

Ahh ... doing stuff. That sounded great, whatever it was. Maybe she was only talking about helping her dad rearrange the stock of toilet rolls and tins of beans out in the back of his shop, but it sounded like heaven to me. Anything except babysitting obnoxious relations. (One of whom was not only nosey, but was also – I'd just spotted – wearing chipped nail varnish of a suspiciously mauvey colour. Looked like the exact same colour as the bottle that had been mysteriously spilt in my room…)

"Have you just been hanging out with your uncle and cousins, then, Al?"

"Yeah, that's right," I replied, not saying anything more while Carli was ogling me through the wooden struts. I tried giving her a go-away glare, but unlike a normal human who'd find that embarrassing and look in the opposite direction, old elf-features Carli just kept right on staring.

"So, what have you done today?"

"Not much," I replied, whirling around with the phone so I was facing away from my horrid cousin. "Just stayed at home with Tor."

Yep, me and Tor had another blissful afternoon on our own – Dad had taken a half-day off work to go and play a game of golf with Uncle Joe (my uncle's idea – Dad probably wouldn't know which end of a club to hold), and Auntie Pauline had taken Charlie and Carli shopping in the West End – to Hamley's toy store, to be exact. Tor and I hadn't been invited, and I can safely say we were thrilled about that. It was just a pity they hadn't stayed out longer: at the sound of Auntie Pauline's "Yoo-hoo!" twenty minutes ago, all the pets vamoosed to far-flung, Charlie-proof corners of the house. All except Spartacus the tortoise, whose short, squat legs couldn't carry him that fast (but at least he had his own portable hidey-hole on his back).

"Well, listen – I don't know if you can come, 'cause of your relatives and everything," Chloe chattered on, "but I'm having everyone round for a girls' sleepover tomorrow night. Mum's taken my brothers to visit my nan and Dad sleeps like a log, so it should be a laugh. Do you fancy it?"

Fancy it? Dead right, I fancied it! *Course* I'd be there, even if it took all my powers of begging and a cross-my-heart-and-hope-to-die promise that I'd devote every second of the next week to The Other Loves. Dad would go for that, wouldn't he? After all, Linn and Rowan were hardly around, so I think I deserved time off for good behaviour.

"Shouldn't be a problem! What time do you want me to come round?" I asked, as I noticed a nervous Winslet stealthily tiptoe out from under the chair in the living room and approach the hall. (I tell you, she looked ridiculous in that muzzle

Uncle Joe and Auntie Pauline insisted she wore – like a small, hairy Hannibal Lecter.)

"What time should everyone come round, d'you think, Sandie?" I heard Chloe's voice go fuzzy as she turned away from the phone.

"Sandie?" I frowned, just as my aunt strolled out of the kitchen with a pair of Marigolds on and Winslet went scuttling back under the chair. "Is Sandie there?"

"Yeah – she's been here all week. Y'know, with her house getting done up and my mum away, it's been a laugh having her stay over. Hasn't it, Sand? What? Oh … Sandie says hi!"

"Hi back," I mumbled, feeling kind of hurt that my best friend was having so much of a laugh without me. No wonder she'd never called me back … she hadn't been home to get any of my messages.

"Well, come about eight o'clock, Ally – and you don't have to bring anything. I'll wangle lots of crisps and stuff off Dad!"

"OK. See you tomorrow, then. Bye…"

Maybe I was still reeling a little from hurt when I put the phone down, but that changed pretty smartly to stunned surprise when I saw what my aunt was up to.

"What are you doing?" I burst out.

"Just a little bit of tidying up!" she said brightly, stretching up and yanking at the party streamers Rowan had lovingly Blu-tacked to the hall ceiling last Saturday. "Your father won't let us contribute anything for staying here, so I just want to help out with some chores around the place."

"But Rowan only just put those up!"

"Yes, Ally, but come *on* now – look at them!" Auntie Pauline lectured me, with a condescending smirk on her bony (elfin?) face. "These ... *things*; they're just hanging messily and attracting dust!"

She was talking to me as if I was incredibly stupid and had rice pudding for brains. So I was very glad that Grandma – accompanied by Linn, who she'd met on the way home – chose that moment to open the front door, which swung wide and nearly sent Auntie Pauline flying.

"Oh, I'm sorry!" said Grandma, with a smile that faded to a frown when she saw the rubber gloves my aunt was wearing and the handful of streamers she was clutching.

"What's going on?" Linn asked cheerfully, hanging her silky, black cardigan up on the coat rack.

"Mummy's tidying up the mess!" Carli trumpeted proudly from behind me on the stairs.

"What – Rowan's dopey streamers?" Linn

laughed. "At least they're not as stupid as this towel she's stapled to the floor!"

Linn kicked a flapping corner of the beach towel Rowan had fixed to the welcome mat, and I felt like kicking her. Didn't she see she was playing into Auntie Pauline's hands? But then Linn's biggest moan about our house was the general clutter about the place. Oh, no – don't say she and Auntie Pauline had something in common at last...

"Yes, that towel! Exactly, Linn! I was just telling Ally that I want to help out around the house to say thank you to your father for letting us stay. And that's my next job – getting rid of that *silly* towel. I mean, any one of the children could trip and injure themselves on it! It's just a hazard, isn't it, Irene?"

I felt like turning round and asking Carli to test that theory out for us, but instead, I looked at Grandma – mess-hater extraordinaire – to see what she made of Auntie Pauline's interference.

"Well, I'm sure Martin would appreciate the thought, Pauline, but as his guests, I'm very sure that he wouldn't want you to be doing any housework!"

Tactfully put, Grandma. Translated from Diplomat, that comes out as "Leave everything alone, you interfering busybody!", if I'm not very much mistaken.

"I'm just glad someone else realizes we live in a tip!" Linn laughed, bending over to tug at the towel.

Good grief – could my big sister just wake up and see how disloyal she was being?

"Well, Irene, I don't know where this one got her sense from, but it certainly wasn't either of her parents!" Auntie Pauline smiled fondly at Linn's bowed head. "She may have her mother's looks but thank goodness she doesn't have her dizziness, eh?"

Hurrah for Auntie Pauline, she had reached a new level of tactlessness! Hadn't it occurred to her that she was talking about Grandma's own daughter? Still, at least that particularly thought-less remark reminded Linn – presently looking gobsmacked – whose side she was supposed to be on...

Chapter 11

CURSE OF THE COUSIN

"I thought I told you you didn't have to bring anything with you?" said Chloe, pulling the front door open.

She was dressed in her PJs, already getting into the spirit of the sleepover, even though it was only eight o'clock.

"Sorry, Chloe," I mumbled, walking into the flat empty-handed (apart from my pyjamas and toothbrush) but dragging an unwelcome cousin in my wake.

"My name's Carli. I come from Canada. In Canada we all live in nice, new houses. Nobody lives above a shop."

Carli had been particularly unimpressed by the dingy alley we'd had to walk up to get to the flat's main entrance at the back of the row of shops. Like I cared.

"Just ignore her," I muttered under my breath to Chloe.

After all, Carli lived in some posh suburb and

100

hadn't got a clue about the real world. I'd already realized from the petty rubbish my cousin and the rest of her family regularly trotted out that The Other Loves lived in an air pocket of small-mindedness that had nothing at all to do with Toronto or the rest of Canada. In fact, the whole of Canada probably had a big old party the moment their plane left the tarmac for Britain. Their prime minister or president or whatever probably declared a day's holiday in celebration of them leaving. And it would probably be a national day of mourning when they arrived back in just over a week's time with their smug, superior smirks and elfy faces.

"Um … what exactly is she doing here, Ally?"

Chloe was eyeing up Carli as if I'd brought along a particularly nasty strain of smallpox to the sleepover.

"It's a long story," I shrugged.

I didn't really want to go into it; not in front of Carli. In fact it was a *short* story – of complete blackmail. Last night, when we were all sitting having tea together (a real *joy*, considering Rowan had just walked into find half her holiday-themed handiwork had been dismantled), I asked Dad if it was OK for me to go to Chloe's sleepover. If I'd had a brain that was half-working, I might have sussed out it would be a better idea to wait till I could get Dad on my own (fat chance of *that* happening in our overpopulated house). So anyway, I asked Dad, Dad said fine, and next thing I knew Carli piped up, "I'd *love* to go to a sleepover, Mummy!" Can you guess what happened next?

"You could have phoned me to say you were bringing her," said Chloe, in her usual, blunt way.

"Sorry," I winced apologetically.

(Translation: "Sorry, my aunt twisted my arm – 'You don't mind, do you, Ally, dear?' – but I was scared to phone and warn you 'cause I knew you be as hacked off about it as I am.")

"Better come in, then," Chloe shrugged, ushering us both inside the flat – which is *huge*, by the way, even if you do have to walk up a dingy alley to get to it. "We're going to be sleeping in the TV room. Me and Sandie spent all day dragging mattresses through and getting it ready!"

As soon as I stepped into the mattress-strewn room, I was met by a chorus of "Hi"s from the rest of my friends, followed by a chorus of "Oh..."s when they caught sight of Carli's sullen face. God, why did she want to come along tonight anyway, if she was just going to be miserable?

"This is my cousin, Carli," I mumbled. "Carli, that's Sandie, who you met before. That's Salma, that's Jen and that's Kellie."

"I'm from Canada. In Canada we—"

"Carli, the bathroom's right across the hall if you want to go and get changed into your pyjamas," Chloe interrupted.

With her usual lack of enthusiasm, Carli turned and mooched off in the direction of the loo.

"Is that all she says? Does she come with a battery we could take out?" Chloe frowned, before flopping herself down on a mound of mismatching duvets and sleeping bags.

"I *wish*..." I mumbled, kicking my trainers off into a corner and getting comfy.

The room looked great – like one massive bed covered in crisps and girls. All of them were already in their pyjamas: Sandie in her Little Mermaid get-up, Jen in a blue gingham top'n'shorts set; Salma in a long, scarlet nightie, Kellie in an old T-shirt and leggings and Chloe all in white – I could guarantee that would have chocolate and Coke stains on it by the end of the night.

"How's it been going?" Sandie mouthed at me, in case old radar-ears could pick us up in the bath-room. (Wouldn't put it past her...) Sandie said it with such concern that I couldn't bring myself to be bugged any more by her hanging out with Chloe all week.

"Terrible!" I whispered back, shutting the door

behind me. "I'm *so* sorry I had to bring her – I couldn't get out of it!"

"It's OK, we'll just carry on like she's not here," Salma shrugged.

"Wish *I* could do that! But we've got her and my uncle and everyone staying for another whole week!"

"Poor you!" Jen scrunched up her face in sympathy.

"*Tell* me about it. It's like—"

"What are we going to do first?" came a voice by my side, all of a sudden.

Carli – the quickest clothes-changer in the West.

"My turn, I guess," I said to the others, ignoring Carli and walking towards the bathroom with my PJs.

"What are we going to do first?" I heard Carli repeat as I went out into the hall.

"We're going to watch videos," I heard Chloe reply.

"What kind of videos?"

"Well, *this* one's a comedy and then for later there's a horror."

"My mummy doesn't let me watch horror movies. My mummy says—"

I shut the bathroom door and slammed the lock shut.

Good grief. Thanks to elf-face in there, this was

quite possibly going to be the *least* fun sleepover me and my friends had ever had.

How wrong can you be?

I was having the best laugh I'd had in ages. The Jim Carrey movie was a scream, the stories Chloe started telling us about her mad relatives in Ireland had us in fits (specially the one about her cousin Declan who went skinny-dipping in the sea and got his clothes washed away by the tide), and the horror film turned out to be so bad it was hysterical.

And now? It was late (really late), we'd eaten everything in the house, and we were still going strong.

"Am I ... a girl?"

Everyone exploded into sniggers. Everyone except Sandie, who grinned broadly at us all, and Carli, who'd thankfully fallen asleep in the corner.

"I guess that means no. OK ... so I'm a boy, then?" said Sandie, and got us all giggling like crazy again.

We were playing that game that no one knows the name of; the one where you secretly write down the name of a famous person on a piece of paper, stick it on your mate's forehead, and get her to guess who it is she's supposed to be by asking you questions. The girls had done it to me first, and

I'd guessed I was Kylie Minogue in the space of four questions ("Am I female?", "Am I famous?", "Do I sing?", "Do I pose with my bum sticking out all the time?"). Then it was Jen's turn, and how she guessed she was Robbie Williams I'll never know ("Am I a boy?" "Am I Robbie Williams?"). After that fluke, it was Sandie's turn and the reason it seemed so hysterical was that sweet, blue-eyed Sandie was sitting huddled up with her Little Mermaid top pulled down over her knees, but had the name "Godzilla" stuck to her forehead.

"Well, if I'm not a girl, and I'm not a boy, am I an animal?" Sandie blinked her big eyes at us.

"Yes!" we all roared so loud that Carli twitched in her sleep (but thankfully didn't wake up).

"Am I something cuddly and fluffy?"

We were laughing so hard that it took Chloe's dad a couple of attempts to be heard.

"Girls!" he called out from the doorway. "What about calling it a night? Or a *morning*, I should say. Some of us have to open a shop tomorrow, you know!"

"You don't open till eleven on Sundays, Dad!" Chloe grinned cheekily.

"Right, you lot, the lights are going out in exactly five seconds' time," Mr Brennan announced firmly. "One … two … three…"

We all squealed like mad and wriggled under the nearest available quilt, scrabbling with other hands that were trying to do the same.

"...four ... five. Goodnight, girls!"

"Goodnight, Mr Brennan!" we all giggled in unison in the dark.

And it *had* been a good night, the best night in ages. Even Carli had been all right – well, she'd watched the movies, eaten the crisps, stayed silent while we yakked, and fallen asleep early, and that was the best I could have hoped for, I guess.

It was almost like being on holiday; on holiday from the Family From Hell...

Chapter 12

THE STRANGE CASE OF THE TAPED-UP TORTOISE

One week's not that long. It's not like it's exactly eternity or anything. Seven short days (not counting today); 168 hours (approximately 63 of them asleep). Yep, I can handle that; I can handle my Relatives From Hell for just that tiny bit of time – no problem.

Those were my thoughts as me and Carli set off yawning for home from Chloe's on Sunday morning. I was still buzzing from last night's silliness, and – get this – I was feeling slightly less frosty towards my cousin. In fact, you could almost say lukewarm. (Don't faint with shock, now.) She hadn't shown me up in front of my friends, and she'd even managed to behave herself, in an invisible kind of a way. I'd been expecting much worse, and been more than pleasantly surprised.

"So, what do you reckon to your first sleepover, then, Carli?"

"It was quite good," she replied, staring off into the gift shop windows we were passing.

"What was the best bit?"

All I got in response to that question was a shrug. But I didn't mind. Carli and I were never going to bond like sisters, but bumbling along pleasantly would do for me. Maybe she was starting to like me, specially now she'd seen me fooling around with all my friends. Maybe she realized that I was an OK person, and that's why she'd started to act like a halfway decent (if quiet) human last night. I'm not the sort of person to hold a grudge – if Carli was going to be nicer to me, then I was more than happy to be nicer to her.

"Your friend Salma – she's really pretty," Carli suddenly piped up conversationally.

"Yes, she is, isn't she?" I nodded, basking in the compliment, even if it wasn't anything to do with me directly.

"Chloe's funny."

"Yeah, she tells good stories."

"Jen's got really piggy little eyes…"

Right, maybe I needed to stop her there, before she said something that made my good intentions towards her melt away quicker than snow that Rolf's weed on.

"So, what are your friends like back home, Carli?"

And that was the conversation the rest of the way back to my place – Carli wittering on about her buddies, or rather *boasting* about her buddies ("Sasha *only* wears designer clothes!", "Laurie's mum and dad have a holiday cottage in Georgian Bay *and* they've got a boat") but it was OK. In fact, everything was OK: the sun was shining, we had a day out planned at London Zoo (the whole family, minus Rowan but plus Grandma), and Dad was going to be proud of his friendly, sociable, dependable daughter.

Dad's friendly, sociable, dependable daughter disappeared as soon as I got home, to be replaced by Dad's agitated, uptight and angry daughter.

But who could blame me, when Tor was so upset? And the fact that Uncle Joe was laughing at him didn't exactly help...

"He *did* do it!" I heard Tor's stressed-out yelp from the kitchen, as soon as me and Carli had got through the front door.

"Calm down, Tor, no harm done!" Uncle Joe was chortling.

I dived into the kitchen, dumping my bag down on the way, and found my brother standing red-faced in the middle of the room, holding up Exhibit A: one tortoise, with a towering Lego house Sellotaped on to the top of its shell.

Uncle Joe, Auntie Pauline and cousin Charlie

were all sitting around the table casually munching toast, oblivious to the obvious fury Tor was trying to express.

"It could *hurt* him!" Tor blasted out, as Spartacus's four claw-like legs scrabbled in the air, searching for *terra firma*.

"Ha, ha, ha! Don't be silly, little fella! It's got a shell as hard as rock! God, Pauline, he's a real softie like his old man, isn't he? Ha, ha!"

"What's going on? Where's Dad?" I asked, dropping to my knees beside Tor and immediately starting to pick away at the tape stuck around the tortoise in our charge.

"Don't panic!" Uncle Joe chuckled, his big, round face beaming as if he'd just heard the funniest joke in the world. "Your dad's just gone for the Sunday newspapers, and Tor here was getting himself into a bit of a state over nothing."

"It's not nothing! And *he* did it!" Tor growled, pointing directly at Charlie, as I gently took Spartacus out of his hands.

"Now, now, Tor," said Auntie Pauline, delicately dipping her knife into the butter, when she should have been hugging my brother or strangling her son or something as far as I was concerned. "We can get this cleared up very quickly. Charlie – did you, or did you not tape Lego to that tortoise?"

Charlie slouched back in his chair with grease and crumbs all around his horrible, sneaky elf face, and blinked innocently at his mother.

"No, Mummy. I didn't do it."

"Now, see, Tor? Glad *that's* settled!"

I narrowed my eyes at my aunt and couldn't help what came out next, even if it was rude. But then everyone *else* was being rude, so why should *I* be left out?

"Well, how is it supposed to have got there? Did the tortoise stick it on himself?"

Uncle Joe began roaring with laughter, which was only more maddening.

"The animal was out in the garden – it was probably some neighbour's children!" Auntie Pauline shrugged.

The neighbours' children? Michael the vet and Harry lived on one side of us (with no children), so I guess it *could* have been the neighbours on the other side, except it would be a miracle since their little boy hadn't started *crawling* yet. Maybe it was the people over the back wall – *their* daughter might have been to blame, but then I was pretty sure, being a trainee policewoman, that it wasn't exactly her thing...

"Anyway, how's my darling Carli?" Auntie Pauline suddenly switched the conversation, while

Uncle Joe wiped the tears of laughter from his big, fat cheeks. "Did you have a good time last night?"

Carli – whom I'd completely forgotten about – slunk around beside her mother and cuddled into her side, as if she was toddler, not a grown-up girl.

"They *made* me watch a horror movie," she blurted out, in a twee little voice.

I was digesting this particular nugget my cousin had come out with, when I caught sight of the shocked and stunned glare my aunt had just given me.

But before either of us had a chance to say anything, Carli blurted out more.

"I was really scared. And then they were all talking about boys, and Ally's friend was talking about a naked boy!"

What naked boy? I thought, my mind scrambling to make sense of what she'd just said, while my fingers struggled to free themselves of the Sellotape tangle they were in.

Declan … was that who Carli was on about? Did she mean Chloe's funny story; the one where her cousin went skinny-dipping in the sea?

"Ally! I *trusted* you to look after Carli!" Auntie Pauline blasted off at me, clattering her knife down on her plate. "I didn't expect you to expose her to this kind of thing!"

Unfortunately, my brain was so frazzled with rage at the injustice of the whole thing that I couldn't think of anything to say except "*Aaaaaaarrrrghhh!*", and I didn't really suppose that would convey my side of the story too well.

And then my uncle seemed to come to my rescue.

"Hold on, Pauline! Don't get mad at the girl!"

Wow – was he really taking my side? Answer: *no*.

"I mean," he continued, "it's not *her* fault if she's a bit off the rails! Look at the role model she's got with that mother of hers, packing up and leaving her kids behind!"

I felt Tor take the now-freed tortoise back out of my sticky hands. I think he was worried that I might throw it at someone...

"Shush! Here comes your father!" said Auntie Pauline, suddenly widening her eyes at both me and Tor as the key rattled in the front door lock. "Let's say nothing more about your bad behaviour, you two – your poor father's got enough on his plate!"

When my "poor" father walked into the room, he could tell straight away that something was up.

"What's going on here?" he smiled warily.

"Oh, we're all just chatting about which animals we want to see at the zoo today!" Auntie Pauline said brightly, while Carli and Charlie both tilted their heads angelically and rested them on their mother's shoulders. "Isn't that right, kids?"

While her own children nodded enthusiastically at her fib, Tor looked long and hard at me. I wondered if we were thinking the same thing – that me, him and all the pets should move out to the shed till the Relatives From Hell left.

Either that, or we were both wondering whether the lions at London Zoo might fancy a light snack of aunt, uncle and poisonous elves...

EARWIGGING AND ARGUMENTS

"Pants."

It was Sunday night, me and my sisters were scooping up a mound of dirty plates from the kitchen table, and I'd just asked Ro how her new summer job was going. By her reply, I could tell she wasn't exactly loving it.

"But isn't it a pretty … well, *trendy* hairdresser's?" Linn asked her.

Linn was right; it absolutely was. I'd passed the shop loads of times when I'd been down at Camden Market, and it definitely wasn't the sort of place your granny goes to get a nice shampoo and set. Not unless she's a really hip, pierced, goth granny, of course.

"Yeah, I guess," Rowan shrugged, making the fat cupid on her shoulder (today's tattoo) jiggle up and down. "But there's nothing very trendy about spending eight hours solid sweeping bits of hair off the floor and washing dirty cups like *I* did all day today."

God, I'd have *happily* spent all day sweeping mangy hair and washing mangier cups – it sounded infinitely preferable to dragging myself around the zoo (no offence to the animals) with the Relatives From Hell. Rowan should count herself lucky.

"Think of the money you're making, Ro! Think of all the hair dye and fake tattoos you can buy!" Linn teased her, eyeing up the lurid fat cupid.

"Who cares about the money?" said Rowan, clattering her pile of dishes down into the sink. "As long as it keeps me away from these stupid relatives of ours!"

"Hear, hear..." muttered Linn.

I knew Rowan was personally smarting from having come home tonight after a hard day's sweeping and mug-washing to find that even *more* of her cheery holiday tat had been "tidied" away by Auntie Pauline. And amazing as it was to hear my sisters agreeing with each other for once, I did have one *tiny* little problem with what they were saying.

"Hey! How do you think me and Tor feel?" I burst out. "*We* don't have jobs to escape to! And you've even managed to move out, Linn – me and Tor are on twenty-four-hour duty, since we've got to share our rooms with Carli and Charlie too! And that's going to be pretty hard for Tor tonight, after what Charlie did to the tortoise today, and the way

Uncle Joe and Auntie Pauline just laughed at him!"

Linn and Rowan stopped and stared open-mouthed at me as I had my mini rant.

It made me feel kind of dizzy, if you want to know the truth, blasting off at my two big sisters like that. But that's the way it was – maybe they didn't mean it but they were both copping out as far as The Other Loves were concerned and not giving me or Tor a passing thought.

"And aren't the four of us supposed to be in this together?" I carried on, all fired up. "I thought we'd *all* decided to try really hard to bite our lips so Dad doesn't realize how bad it is. But it's pretty hard for me and Tor to keep secrets on our own, the way you two keep schlepping off!"

Linn didn't say anything straight away; she just stepped across to the door – past where the banana-framed poster of Croatia had hung until today – and pushed it closed.

"It wasn't my idea to move out, you know, Ally," she told me, sitting down at the kitchen table and leaning her elbows in the crumbs.

"I know," I mumbled, sitting down opposite her. "But you've only seen a little bit of what they're like."

"Enough to know they're awful," Linn grinned at me.

"Yeah, but that's just *normal* awful – they save that for you and Dad and Grandma. Me and Tor, we've seen them when they're *super*-awful."

"I've been around for that too, Al!" Rowan reminded me, slinking into another chair and looking hurt. Even the fat cherub seemed to be moping.

"OK, that's it," said Linn, slapping her hands down on the table. "We've *got* to tell Dad what's going on."

"But we said we wouldn't! We said we'd put up with it for Dad's sake!" Rowan said in alarm.

"Yeah, but he doesn't know how bad it's getting, does he?" Linn pointed out. "So, I *definitely* think we should say something!"

It was great having Linn come over all decisive (normally I'd call it bossy). I'd missed that – in a funny way I'd felt quite lonely in this packed house all week without her around.

"But how do we let him know without upsetting him?" asked Rowan.

"Or sounding like we're whingeing telltales?" I added, since I'd had *quite* enough of tale-telling this last week.

Linn frowned, deep in thought.

"I wish there was some way Dad could see them at their worst, then we wouldn't even have to say anything. It'd just be obvious!"

"But how could we do that?" I asked. "Do you mean we *tape* them or something?"

Stanley mentioned once that he had a video camera, but I don't think Grandma would be too thrilled if we borrowed that for the purposes of blackmail. Even though it would be brilliant to catch Carli helping herself to my nail varnish and whatever else in my room when she thought no one was looking.

"Not *tape* them," Linn shook her head. "I don't know ... if there was some way we could *push* them into behaving really badly in front of Dad. That's all we'd need to do."

I think it must have been round about then that I heard a Something, but I was way too interested in what Linn was saying to pay any attention to what my ears were trying to tell me.

Bad move.

"You mean, if we deliberately started acting up a bit, so Uncle Joe and Auntie Pauline came out with more of that stuff about how badly Mum brought us up?" I suggested, since the slagging off of Mum was what was particularly winding me up today.

"Maybe," shrugged Linn.

"I've got it!" Rowan grinned. "We lock Charlie in a room with Rolf and a can of spray-on cream for five minutes – then we make Dad open the door, and I guarantee there'll be one sticky dog and one guilty kid!"

"Yeah! Let's see Uncle Joe and Auntie Pauline try and deny that!" I giggled, imagining Rolf with white peaks down his back, like a furry mountain range.

"And then when they start making excuses for their precious son," said Linn, "we all do like Ally says and argue back a bit. That'll start one of them going on about Mum's terrible influence!"

"Do you think we should get Tor in on this?" asked Ro, eyes wide with excitement at our cunning plan.

"Ahem."

That "ahem" – it came from the kitchen door-way, and it came from the disapproving mouth of our gran. The Something I heard a few seconds ago; it sounded like a creaky floorboard squeaking in the hall as Someone walked towards this room. Uh-oh...

"I don't know what silly games you girls are up to, but I don't expect you or your brother to be involved in any nonsense when it comes to your visitors. All right?"

"But Grandma," Linn started trying to explain, "we were just—"

"—acting a lot younger than you are," said Grandma sternly.

"But, Grandma, it's not like that," Rowan tried to explain next, realizing – like me and Linn – that our gran had just caught us fooling around with our plan to frame The Other Loves, and not heard the reason *why* we were trying to frame them. "We were only—"

"I don't want to hear any explanations, Ro. I realize that it's hard for people to get along when they haven't much in common and when they're living in such close proximity, but I'd certainly be very disappointed to think my grandchildren were being in any way rude or badly behaved in front of guests. I'm sure that would hurt your father very much."

Ouch.

Grandma gave us all a cool look through her gold-rimmed glasses; the sort of cool look that makes you shrivel down till your neck disappears somewhere into your collarbone.

"Let's not say another word about this. Linn – I was thinking it was about time we were leaving."

"OK…" Linn murmured, giving me and Rowan a quick glance before she left, pink-cheeked, to get her jacket.

"Bye, girls," Grandma nodded in our direction.

"Bye," Rowan and I mumbled, feeling well and truly told off.

"So I guess we dump the plan, then?" said Rowan, once we'd heard Grandma and Linn say their farewells to everyone in the living room, and made out the sound of the front door clicking shut.

"I guess so."

"Guess we're just going to have to shut up and put up with that lot, aren't we?"

"Guess so."

"Do you want to wash or dry?"

"Huh?"

I turned to see that Rowan was holding up a tea towel in one hand and rubber gloves in the other, trying to act normal even though she looked as down as I felt.

"I'd rather dig a big hole in the garden and get right in it," I shrugged. "But I'll do the drying. You get started – I'm going to the loo first."

"You're not going to try and get out of it by drowning yourself up there, are you?" Ro managed a wan smile as I went out the kitchen door.

"With our wonky plumbing? I'd have to wait two weeks for the bath to fill up enough to drown myself!"

Ah, well. We were still going to have to share our house with the Relatives From Hell for another

123

week, and our gran was ashamed at us for being juvenile and rude. But as long as me and Rowan could joke around a little bit, I might just stay sane till next Sunday. Maybe...

There was a flurry of disappearing cats from the hall stairs as I began tiptoeing up towards the loo, then a brave face or two peeked back down at me through the bannisters when they realized I was friend, not foe. (Eddie in particular hadn't enjoyed wearing the blue suit and black cap that had spookily transferred itself from Tor's Postman Pat toy to his own furry body yesterday...)

Then – on the first-floor landing – I heard voices, and hesitated outside Tor's bedroom door, peering in through the gap where the cosy warmth from his bedside lamp spilled out. What story was he listening to tonight, I wondered?

But the only story going on was coming from Tor's own lips.

"...and I didn't know where he was, but then I found him out in the garden, like *this*!"

Tor was holding up a floppy black and white something. I squinted for a split second and realized it was Mr Penguin, one of Tor's favourite stuffed toys. Only he was missing most of his stuffing by the looks of it, as well as one eye.

"And you think Charlie did it?" asked Dad,

sitting crossed-legged on the floor beside Tor's lilo bed.

Tor nodded hard. "He's horrible – they're *all* horrible."

Yikes – it looked like my brother was spilling the beans, which was a lot more straightforward than the plan me and my sisters had tried to concoct downstairs. What was Dad going to make of that?

"You really think so, Tor?"

We all do, Dad, we all do! I felt like yelling. But I'd let Tor have his moment first.

"Uncle Joe's always *hitting* you."

"It's not really *hitting* hitting, Tor," Dad tried to explain. "It's just his way of being friendly!"

"He's a big *bully*..." Tor mumbled, dropping his gaze to his dolphin-covered duvet.

"Oh, Tor, your uncle Joe's not a bully! He's just a bit ... um, *loud*," Dad sighed.

Loud; that was right. Like today, when he'd deliberately ignored the sign not to do it and made stupid LOUD monkey noises at the gorillas. They went totally *mad*, rattling the wire walls of their compound cages and jumping around all over the place till a zookeeper came hurrying over and told Uncle Joe to quit it (Uncle Joe just laughed). And then there was Friday night, when he went around the house hollering, "I am the CHAMPION of the

WORLD!" about fifty times, all because he'd won the game of golf he'd played with Dad. Of course some people (like me) might say that winning a golf game isn't that hard when you're an expert and your brother knows as much about golf as he does about brain surgery, but that didn't stop Uncle Joe whooping and yelping and doing lots of bruise-inducing thumping on Dad's arm all through tea.

"Listen, Tor, I *promise* I'll have a word with Uncle Joe and Auntie Pauline about Charlie and Mr Penguin—"

"And Spartacus and the Lego."

So Tor had told him about that too…

"*And* Spartacus and the Lego—"

"And Eddie and Postman Pat's clothes."

"*And* Eddie and Postman Pat's clothes."

"And Winslet and the tumble dryer."

"*And* Winslet and the tumble dryer—"

"And—"

"And all the others, Tor, I know. I will *definitely* sort it out," Dad said soothingly. "But here's the thing…"

Ooh … what was the thing? I wondered, trying not to breathe too loudly and disturb Dad and Tor's tête-à-tête. (Posh French for cosy chat. I'm dead cultured, me.)

"The thing is," Dad continued, looking all apologetic, "you know how much you love your sisters, and you love having them around?"

I watched as Tor nodded solemnly, while patting Rolf's head, which had just poked out from under the bed.

"Well, you'd be sad if you didn't get to see them very often, wouldn't you, Tor?"

Cue more silent nodding of the small brother variety.

"Well, sometimes I get a bit sad that Uncle Joe lives so far away from us and that I can't see him when I want to."

"Oh," I heard Tor mutter.

Oh, I thought, hovering out on the landing and feeling my sense of injustice slip-slide away.

"So, as a *big* favour to me – while I'm trying to get to know my big brother a bit better – can you just try *really* hard to put up with Charlie and everything? Just for a *few* more days? If I absolutely promise to have a word with Uncle Joe and get things sorted out?"

When Dad put it like that, I suddenly felt like the meanest, most selfish daughter in the world. Ro was right; even if having the Relatives From Hell staying *was* as much fun as having your eyelashes tugged out with tweezers, it was important for Dad to get a chance to hang out with the brother he hadn't seen in ages. Even if it did mean bruises.

So, five minutes later, when Dad came into the kitchen and put the kettle on with a cheery smile, he found me right beside Ro, tea towel in my hand, trying – once again – to think myself into being a very thoughtful daughter indeed.

And then I heard the fight.

OK, so it wasn't exactly a fight, but Dad was certainly sounding annoyed, and mostly that seemed to be because Uncle Joe was laughing at him. (Does that sound familiar...?)

Everyone else was fast asleep: Carli was snuggled in my bed, dreaming dreams of how to be sneaky and two-faced (probably); Charlie was snoozing in Tor's bed, dreaming dreams of new tortures for our pets (very probably); Tor was fitfully napping, having nightmares about pets being tortured (very, very probably) and Rowan was unconsciously drifting in glitter-twinkling Rowan-Land, where her hair was black and waist-length and a string of fairy lights was tattooed around her upper arm (almost definitely). Auntie Pauline? Well, I could hear her snoring like a very snorey pig in Dad's room when I popped down to get a glass of water.

"But Tor's only seven! It really upsets him if anything happens to any of the animals!" I heard Dad say as I crept downstairs, past a slumbering cat or three, and positioned myself on the bottom step – a good vantage point for peering through the crack in the living-room doorway and listening in. (For the *second* time today. I should ask the careers advisor at school for information on what qualifications you need to become a spy. Ally Love, agent 007-and-a-half...)

"Ha, ha, ha! Come *on*, Martin! See the funny side! Even if it *is* Charlie, he's only having a laugh! No one's getting hurt!"

I couldn't see my dad or my uncle's face from where I was – sorry, where *we* were (Winslet had just joined me) – but I saw Uncle Joe's arm bend down and pick up a bottle of beer from the coffee table. Make that the *beer* table judging by the number of empty bottles on it. Dad and Uncle Joe were obviously making a bit of a night of it.

"But *Tor*'s getting hurt, and what about Charlie? He nearly got hurt too, when he tried to stick Winslet in the dryer!"

At the mention of her name in the same sentence as Charlie's, Winslet let out a long, low growl. I put a hand over her mouth (and muzzle) to shut her up.

"Martin, that boy of yours is too soft. Don't get me wrong – I know why you and the girls spoil him, but just because Melanie took off doesn't mean you have to—"

"Leave Melanie out of this!" I heard Dad say agitatedly. "But while we're on the subject of wives, it's bad enough that yours is wandering around the house taking down all the summer decorations that the kids spent so much time on—"

"Ah, now, Martin – Pauline's only trying to help straighten this place up a bit, as a gesture!"

"Well, me and the kids like our tip of a house just the way it is, Joe, and since Pauline doesn't ever take the hint when I've mentioned it to her, I'd appreciate it if you could let her know that if I see *one* more poster taken down or hear *one* more dig about our home looking tatty, then you can find an overpriced bucket of a hotel like you suggested in the first place!"

"Chill out, Martin! What are you getting so worked up about?"

"What ... what I'm *really* getting worked up about," I heard my dad bluster, "is you and your wife's habit of bad-mouthing mine in front of my kids!"

Wow. So much for protecting Dad and hiding stuff from him; it seemed like he knew a *lot* more than we gave him credit for. And, brilliant – he was really letting Uncle Joe have it!

"Pauline? She'd never bad-mouth anyone. You've got it *all* wrong, Martin. She's just concerned for you and your—"

"Look – you *and* her have made little digs in front of me about Melanie, and my mother-in-law's spotted that too."

`Yessss! Go, Dad, go!

"And I just don't want the kids picking up on that any more than they have already – OK, Joe?"

"Hey, hey, *hey*, little brother!" Uncle Joe's voice boomed. "Don't get so *sensitive*! God, you're *all* a bit sensitive! It's all 'cause of Melanie taking off and jaunting around the world, without a backward glance, isn't it?"

"*Joe!*" Dad raged.

"Aww, come on – don't take offence at me, your own brother. C'mere…"

There was a pause, then I heard Dad mumble, "OK."

Winslet and I winced as that "OK" was followed by a loud few *thwack*s, and I could practically *hear* Dad groan under Uncle Joe's overenthusiastic bear-hugging back-thumps.

"And hey – to make it up to you, just to show you we care, how about you go to that bicycle show of yours next week, Martin? Me and Pauline'll take care of the kids. How about that!"

No! I felt like yelping from behind the door.

"No, I couldn't," Dad thrilled me by saying. "I've already cancelled it anyway."

"Well, *un*cancel it!" Uncle Joe laughed. "We're off to see Pauline's relatives tomorrow, but we'll be back here on Wednesday, which means you can go to the show no problem! And we'll still be able to spend Saturday together once you're back, like one big happy family!"

No! *No!*

"I really don't think…"

"I insist, Martin! It's a done deal!"

"I can't…"

"Yes you can! Give me one good reason why you can't!"

Because it'll send us deranged! I shouted inside my head.

"Well, I … I don't know if Rory could cover me for the whole time now, since I mucked him about with changing dates already."

"Phone him and check."

"I suppose I could. But if he can't do it…"

"Then shut the shop for a couple days, Martin. If people need any repairs done, then they can wait till you're back. And you said yourself that this bike fair's important for business, didn't you?"

"Well, I guess so..."

"See? So no more arguments – you're going, right?"

"I suppose I could..."

No! No! *No!*

"Fantastic! So, is this officially a truce?" Uncle Joe bellowed.

Dad must have nodded, 'cause the next thing I could make out was Uncle Joe announcing, "Right, let's toast that with another beer. I'll get 'em in!"

And with that, his footsteps stomped towards the living-room door and the hallway I was ear-wigging in. But by the time he'd yanked the door open, I was already sprinting silently up the second flight of stairs to my attic bedroom, with my fingers tightly crossed that – the hideous new babysitting arrangements aside – this night's conversation would help clear the air and make the *next* week somehow more bearable.

Um ... rearrange the following words into a well known phrase or saying: chance fat...

KYRA AND THE SECRET CODE

Excellent, excellent, excellent.

That's three excellents, if you hadn't noticed, and those three excellent things happen to be…

Excellent thing No. 1) Everyone seemed to be behaving themselves this Monday morning. Auntie Pauline hadn't tidied away anything she shouldn't have, or said anything out of order about Mum (had Dad's chat with Uncle Joe last night done the trick?). Uncle Joe hadn't hit Dad once (he left for the bike shop today thump-free). Carli was keeping her tale-telling mouth shut, and Charlie didn't appear to have taunted any pets between the time he got up and the time he had breakfast, which was amazing really. (Still, the day was young.)

Excellent thing No. 2) The Relatives From Hell were off to visit unfortunate relations in Guildford, and – joy! – they were going to be staying with them for two nights! Bliss…

Excellent thing No. 3) Kyra was back! And after the stressed-out week I'd had (so much for relaxing summer holidays), there was nothing I wanted more than to listen to her tales of sun, sea, Spain and surf-dudes.

See what I mean about excellent?

"What's Tor doing?" asked Kyra, staring out of my attic bedroom down on to the faraway dark head of my little brother, who was hovering about on the pavement beside Uncle Joe's hire car.

"I think he's checking for tortoises," I explained (badly), as I joined her leaning on the window sill with the two Cokes I'd just brought up from the kitchen.

"What – is there a plague of them round here or something?" Kyra joked.

Her skin, I noticed, was a distinctly darker shade of light brown and her freckles were out in force after her week in the Mediterranean sun.

"Just the opposite," I told her. "There's only one tortoise, and it's been missing since last night. I think Tor's checking that none of The Other Loves are packing it in the car with them. But *I* think it's just gone into hiding till the coast's clear – if it's got any sense."

"Wow, things *are* bad if your brother's suspecting *that* lot of tortoise kidnap!"

"Well, he nearly lost Kevin the iguana last week when Charlie tied balloons to him to see if he could get him to fly," I shrugged. "One gust of wind and it could have been bye, bye, Kevin…"

"Pity we don't have balloons now," Kyra drawled, as we both watched Uncle Joe put bags in the back of the car. "We could have filled them with water and bombed your cousins from here…"

"What, and get another lecture off my aunt about what little motherless heathens we are?" I grinned back at her.

It was good to have Kyra back. Her fearlessness was kind of frightening sometimes, but there were times (like this) that it was quite nice to hang out with someone brave and mouthy. Not to mention entertainingly bitchy.

"So … since I've been away," she said, stopping to suck on her straw, "all I've missed is you being driven insane by your rubbish relatives and one sleepover at Chloe's."

"And me getting chucked by Feargal, remember," I added with a heavy heart and a big, fat sigh.

"Ally, I've forgotten that already. I mean, I quite liked him, but the guy's obviously a loser if he dumped you for not knowing anything about hip-hop and having Billy as your mate."

Oh, yes, it was good to have Kyra back. I could feel my deflated ego pumping up nicely already.

"OK, I'll forget him too," I added defiantly.

"Who?" Kyra smirked, shooting me a knowing look from the corner of her eyes.

"Dunno, I've forgotten already," I shrugged, playing along with her. "So come on – tell me more about this guy you met!"

How tantalizing. When Kyra had arrived ten minutes ago, she'd told me about her dad getting stung by a poisonous jellyfish the first day of their holiday, about the flirty waiters in the restaurant they went to most often, and about the tanned German granny who liked to parade topless around the pool ("Droopy? Ally, they were practically down to her *flip*-flops!"). But it was only *after* she'd said all that that she mentioned the family they'd buddied up with; the family with a *very* cute son. And that was *all* she'd say, till she'd heard what had gone on back in Crouch End while she'd been away.

"Well, his name's Sam, he's fourteen, and he's from Wimbledon."

So much for Kyra's dreams about finding herself a Spanish surf-dude.

"And?"

"And?" she teased me, being deliberately annoying (Kyra's speciality).

"*And* did you like him straight away? How cute is he? Did you—"

I was cheerfully rattling through my questions when an icy presence – like a ghost running an ice cube down my spine – alerted me to the fact that we weren't alone...

"All right, Carli?" I said flatly, as my cousin hovered idly in the doorway of my bedroom.

"That cat shouldn't be in here." She nodded in the general direction of Colin, who been contentedly snoozing upside-down on the bed (one fuzzy belly and three legs pointing to the ceiling) till the malicious menace of Carli had disturbed his slumbers.

"No pets in here at *night* – that was the agreement, remember?" I pointed out to her.

Carli said nothing in response; she just rocked back and forth on one leg and stared at me insolently. That was quite surprising, actually. I'd have expected her to be halfway down the stairs by now, running to tell her precious mum that Colin was infecting the bedroom with his general catness and that I didn't care (me being so wildly "off the rails" and everything).

"Um, shouldn't you be down in the car, Carli?"

"Just came for a couple of things," she shrugged, strolling into the room. "And anyway, nobody else is ready to go yet."

Yeah ... your mum's probably just finishing

*peeling Rowan's plastic sun off the living-room
window and Charlie'll be busy pulling the wings off
flies or something,* I thought, as I watched her amble
over to her suitcase and rummage about inside it.

It didn't look like she was in a hurry to move,
from the way she flopped herself crossed-legged
on the floor. Well, tough – she wasn't going to spoil
my time with my friend.

"So, go on," I turned back to Kyra. "You were
telling me about Sam."

"Well," she began, casting a wary sideways
glance at Carli before she carried on. "His family
ended up on this really dull boat trip Mum and
Dad had made me go on, and it turned out brilliant
– his folks started yakking to mine, and then me
and Sam got talking when the boat stopped on this
deserted beach for a barbecue. He's *so* cool – he's
a DJ and everything; he's got his own decks at
home."

I felt like saying, a DJ where exactly? In Club
Bedroom? It wasn't like all the trendy clubs in
London or Ibiza were exactly *gagging* to hire
fourteen-year-old DJs. But I didn't feel like
winding Kyra up – after a week of mind-numbing
hell, I was enjoying her company too much.

"Did you see him just that once? On that trip, I
mean?" I asked instead, taking a slug from my glass

of Coke and feeling the bubbles shoot up my nose.

Bubbles were getting the better of Kyra too, and she let out a deeply unladylike burp before she answered my question.

"*Urrrrpppp!* Oops – 'scuse me! Anyway, no – we hung out every day after that, which was great, 'cause I thought I'd *die* of boredom being stuck with Mum and Dad the whole week. We just mucked around the pool or the beach and had a laugh, even though it was a bit of a drag having his sister tag around with us everywhere."

"How old was she?"

"Nine. And she was dead *nosey*," Kyra said pointedly, throwing a look in Carli's direction.

Carli was doing an excellent job of pretending not to listen in, although I was sure she was – she wasn't fooling me with that routine of endlessly rummaging around in her suitcase, her head bent down behind the opened lid. I decided I'd better try and edit what I was going to say next – specially when there was a question I desperately wanted to ask.

"Did you…"

I paused, wondering if Kyra would get my secret code. Subtlety has never been her thing, and she doesn't have sisters who can slip into secret-code speak at the wink of an eye, like I do. I had to think quick – and then suddenly, I had an idea, inspired by (of all people) my cousin Charlie.

"Did you and Sam..." I began again, then breathed a quick circle of condensation against a pane of glass in my window. With my finger, I wrote "snog", but out loud I said, "...talk?"

For half a second Kyra looked at me and my windowpane doodle and seemed totally bemused. Then she caught on; I could tell from her Cheshire Cat grin.

"Ah...! Did we 'talk'? You *bet* we talked!"

Hurrah! We were getting to the juicy stuff! And Carli hadn't a clue what we were on about!

"When did you first ... erm, *talk*?" I asked her.

"The first day, at the barbecue!"

Kyra – she's a fast worker, that's for sure.

"At the barbecue? You ... *talked* to Sam in front of your *parents*?"

"No! We went for a walk along the beach, miles away from them. And wow, Ally was he a good sno— *talker*!"

"Did you, um, *talk* often?" I tried to stifle a giggle.

"Every day!" Kyra giggled back. "Whenever we could, we *talked* and *talked* and *talked*!"

And then me and Kyra started snickering like idiots; you know, those sort of snickers you get in assembly when the more you try not to laugh, the funnier whatever it is *is*, if you see what I mean.

"Got it!" Carli suddenly announced, holding up a hairslide and crashing the lid of the suitcase so hard that me and Kyra jumped.

"OK, good. Well, have a nice time in Guildford. See you on Wednesday," I said to Carli, feeling a weight rise off my shoulders as my cousin trotted off towards the stairs.

She didn't reply, just stared one of her weird, unreadable elfin stares at me and Kyra, before she disappeared down the stairs.

"She's *freaky*..." mumbled Kyra, in her usual not-very-quiet mumble.

"*Tell* me about it," I whispered back, in a proper whisper. "You just never know what she's thinking or what she's going to come out with next!"

I had never spoken a truer word (or *words*, if you're going to get picky). As we happily chattered on – code-free – about Sam the excellent snogger, I had no idea that Carli was currently telling her mother that me and Kyra had been having some X-rated conversations about "naked ladies" (she must have been listening outside the door before she came to search for her hairslide) and "naughty things with boys". Not to mention the outrageous, uncouth burp-fest she'd been subjected to.

But I found out soon enough, when Auntie Pauline came thundering up the stairs like she'd got a rocket stuck up her bum, hissing that she'd prefer it if me and Kyra wouldn't expose her sweet, naive daughter to such filthy talk in the future…

Erm … excuse me?

And with that, there was a toot from Uncle Joe at the helm of the hire car, and Auntie Pauline (and her poisonous elves) were gone, before I'd even got the chance to stand up for myself.

"Hey, Ally … if Carli's supposed to be so sweet and naive," Kyra frowned, as soon as the front door had slammed shut and we'd shaken ourselves out of shock, "how come she can make up all that seriously *rude* stuff she told her mum?"

"Don't ask me…" I shrugged, going over to grab Colin off the bed for a comforting hug.

All *I* was thinking about was what I'd done in a past life to deserve such a bunch of total *muppets* for relations…

ALIENS AND ICE CREAM

Everybody's always going on about how brilliant school holidays are. But you know, I'm not so sure...

Before you go thinking I'm insane, I'll try and explain what I mean. Yeah, so I love not having to get up early and play beat-the-family-to-the-bathroom (there's always plenty of hot water in our house – for the first three people who use the shower). I love not having to wear my stupid school tie (who invented ties? They don't keep you warm, they don't hold anything up, they don't do *anything* ... useless!). I love not having any maths homework (x+y=my brain melting). And if it's just Easter or half-term then holidays are *bliss*.

But there's something weird about the summer holidays: they're so long that stuff can seriously change in that time. At school, you get to see your best friends every day, but during the holidays everyone drifts off and does different stuff with their families and everything, and sometimes it's like you just don't *fit* together again once the next term starts. Like me and this tomboy girl Beth at primary school; we got to be really close in Year 4, and then she came back at the start of Year 5 as this totally different person. She'd spent four weeks in France and suddenly had an accent, long nails and a penpal called Amelie who she was much more interested in staying in and writing to than rolling down the hill at Ally Pally with me.

I guess that's what was worrying me a bit about *this* summer. Maybe I'd had fun the night of Chloe's sleepover, but the way the girls were talking (including Sandie) they'd all been hanging out together loads (especially Sandie and Chloe) – what if I still felt like an outsider once the Relatives From Hell had flown out of my life? After all, it wasn't looking too promising, if this week was anything to go by – apart from seeing Kyra on Monday morning, I hadn't managed to get together with *any* of my mates; they'd all been too busy with this, that and the other. Now it was late on Wednesday afternoon, Carli and Co were due back any time, and I hadn't done anything much apart from hang out with Tor and search for missing tortoises. And as for my sisters, well, since our telling-off from Grandma on Sunday, we hadn't really done much talking about anything other than "pass the salt" stuff, in an effort to be seen as non-rude, good daughters in front of Dad. All in all, I was feeling pretty lonely, if you want to know...

Speaking of tortoises and grandmothers, Grandma had forced Tor to temporarily call off the search this afternoon and had taken him – and an un-muzzled Winslet and Rolf – to the park for a couple of hours' worth of bounding. She'd asked me to come too, but I was kind of in the mood to stay at home and indulge in a bit of heavy-duty moping (and I didn't feel much like being on my almost own with her since I still felt a bit funny about our fall-out). And once I'd spent a while worrying about being deserted by all my friends and spending a long, lonely life with only cats and a cupboard full of nachos for company, I decided to be gloomy about the fact Dad had left for the bike fair this morning, which meant that soon I'd be forced to spend non-quality time with non-lovely members of my family, while I was hardly seeing – and in Mum's case, *never* seeing – the *truly* lovely members of my family.

Then out of nowhere, I thought of a funny, blurry photo from some summer long ago... It's of me and my sisters and my mum out in the garden, all of us squealing and soaking as Dad sprays us with water from the hose, at the same time as trying to snap us (which explains why the thing's not exactly in focus).

"Wish you were home right now, Mum," I mumbled, opening the door of my wardrobe and searching out my memory box of bits, bobs, odds and ends and (importantly) out-of-focus snapshots. "You'd soon sort Uncle Joe and everyone out!"

And then I realized she wouldn't; Uncle Joe's right, Dad is a softie, and so is Mum. She'd have bitten her lip and counted to ten trillion – like the rest of us were doing, including Dad, despite his argument with Uncle Joe the other night – just to keep the peace. In fact, Dad was guilty of being a total softie again today; right before he left, he let himself be talked into something that's going to please Linn not one tiny bit. My uncle had phoned (from Auntie Pauline's relatives' house in Guildford) and suggested that to keep the peace between Tor and Charlie, Charlie should move into Linn's room while Dad was away for the next three nights. And Dad said yes! I mean, I know he was thinking of Tor (of course) when he did it, but he obviously didn't think about the repercussions for Linn – having her sanctuary invaded by one hyperactive little troll was going to give her a heart attack...

Anyway, that wasn't my problem (I had enough

of those). I was just about to reach for the box when something made me pause. It – the box, I mean – wasn't were it should be, i.e. tucked right at the back, behind a pile of winter boots and favourite trainers I'd grown out of but couldn't bear to throw away. Instead it had been tugged closer, with the lid partly open and a piece of green paper sticking out … the programme from Tor's school play last Christmas, I think it was.

At that point, I gave up the idea of looking for the fuzzy photo I'd wanted to dig out and peered round at the rest of the room instead. Everything was exactly as it should have been: *almost*.

The drawer with my jumpers and cardies in it; I hadn't opened that since the end of winter, but it was ever so slightly open now, with a tiny cuff of something woolly and bobbly jamming the drawer open. The jumble of paper and scribblings and notes I made to myself on my desk – that had suddenly turned into a neatish pile, as if someone had been looking through them and tidied them up in a way that I never would. The few bits of make-up I kept on my dressing table … there was a big fingerprint in the middle of a tub of strawberry-flavoured lip gloss I hadn't used yet. And next to the blob of dried mauve nail varnish I'd spotted before was a smear of powdery blue eyeshadow, along with *more* powdery-blue fingermarks on the lid of the tin where I keep my hairbands and rings and things.

Hey, how would Carli like it if I told tales on *her* to Auntie Pauline? About how she'd obviously been noseying everywhere in my room at every available opportunity? But then, Auntie Pauline would never believe it was Carli who'd meddled with my stuff. She'd accuse Winslet or the tortoise of trying on my eyeshadow before she'd admit her darling daughter had anything to do with it.

"*Hiiiiiiiyyyyyaaaaaaaa!*"

Hurrah – that was Rowan, home from another hard day's mug-washing. I needed a witness to see this, and a very big favour to ask before my head exploded...

"Well, *that* was dumb."

"What was dumb?" I squinted at Billy. The sun was still shining so bright up here on the hill that it could have been noon and not nearly teatime. (My watch was telling me that – not my rumbling tummy, which was presently full of Rocky Road ice cream.)

"Well, how about *first*, you go and tell Rowan that Carli has been going through all your private stuff..."

I nodded, since I could hardly forget the heated

conversation I'd just had with my sister less than half an hour ago.

"...and *then* you go and beg her to let Carli share her room for the next few days!"

OK, I could see his point – I hadn't exactly sold it well to Rowan. Her room is a shrine to all things glittery and knick-knacky ... the idea of having Carli's little elf fingers prying into them all probably made Rowan hyperventilate in panic. But at the time, I just felt like she was being ultra-unfair. After all, out of her and Linn and I, *I* was the one spending the most time with my obnoxious cousin, and since I was the youngest out of all of us, that seemed pretty tough on me (specially since Tor was getting a break at the moment too, now that creepy Charlie had moved into Linn's room). When I was mouthing off to Rowan, I'd really hoped she come over all big sisterly on me and tell me not to worry; to drag Carli's suitcase down to her room, and assure me that she'd take it from there. But then I guess I was confusing Rowan with someone who wasn't a fluff-brained airhead...

"What you *should* have done," Billy waffled on, "is bribed Rowan. That would have been *much* simpler."

"I tried that before. I offered to buy her a new string of fairy lights but she wasn't having it."

"God!" Billy yelped, clutching a hand to the chest of his scruffy T-shirt and faking a coronary at the news. "Is there something *wrong* with her? Is she *ill*?"

"Maybe it's that hair dye she's been using. Maybe it's seeping into her brain and short-circuiting all the twinkly bits."

Ah, it felt good to sit on our trusty old bench and talk rubbish with Billy. He'd been great when I phoned him on the way to the park, all grumpy and flipping out over Rowan's (quite understandable) refusal to share her space with elf-face. Billy had only just got in from a game of football somewhere, but as soon as we spoke, he'd got back on his bike and come and met me up here. My mood switched from miserable to happy as soon as I met up with him. 'Course, maybe that *also* had something to do with the giant tub of Häagen Dazs he'd nicked out of the freezer at home to help cheer me up.

A shoulder to cry (well, moan) on and a mound of medicinal ice cream – that's the sign of a true friend...

"But don't be mad at Rowan, Al – you're probably *all* feeling a bit grumpy and tetchy having those weirdo strangers clogging up your house."

You know, Billy was right (and that's a first).

Uncle Joe, Auntie Pauline, Telltale Carli and Psycho Charlie ... they *were* more like strangers than family; so much for blood being thicker than water. And now I felt *seriously* bad for getting so mad at Ro. I'd have to make it up to her later; I'd get her a new pack of fake tattoos from the newsagent tomorrow.

"You know something?" I mused, wafting my dribbly spoon in the air.

"What's that?" Billy asked, digging another scoop out of the tub we were holding between us.

"Don't you think it's freaky that I love my dad to bits, but I don't love *anything* about my uncle? I mean, they're brothers – you'd think they had *something* in common!"

"Maybe your uncle's an alien. Maybe the whole human thing is just a cover; he was dumped on earth in the guise of a baby, then he married another alien and they had their alien kids. Oh, yeah – those relations of yours are *trouble*. First, they're going to take over Canada, *then* Crouch End, and *then* the WORLD! Omigod, Ally, you *have* to put a stop to their evil plans!"

I was about to tell him he was as nutty as a Snickers bar and to shut up, and then I realized that this might be the last bit of fun I'd have till after Sunday.

"And how do you think I can stop them?" I grinned at him.

Billy fixed me with an intense stare. "Ally, what *you* need is a warp-factor, electron-neutralizing atomic alien vaporizer."

"Oh, yeah?" I replied, arching my eyebrows at him. "And where exactly can I get one of those, then?"

"Woollies, I think," said Billy, quarter of a second before I *ping*ed a dollop of Rocky Road right in his face...

Chapter 16

SECRETS AND BIG EARS

Thursday: Day 12 of the Invasion of the Relatives From Hell, Day 2 of being stuck home alone with them, and Day 4 of the Mysterious Case of the Missing Tortoise.

"Do you like them?"

I was lounging on Rowan's inflatable green chair, with two cats that weren't Colin (Derek and Eddie) curled up in a snurfling, snorey, black and white furry ball on my lap (which was pretty heavy actually – but they looked so comfy and contented that I didn't have the heart to turf them off).

Rowan bounded over from the other side of the room – where she'd been holding a packet of stick-on tattoos up against her newly scrubbed upper arm in the mirror – gave me a squeeze (which made the chair, me and the cat-mass bounce), and flopped down in front of me, studying the present I'd secretly bought for her when we'd been out earlier.

"They're *gorgeous*, Ally! Thank you!"

The £2.99 tattoos I'd treated my sister to from the newsagent were all fairies, apart from one devilish red imp, which I didn't like very much because it reminded me of a couple of elves she and I happened to have the misfortune to be related to. Two elves who were at this moment downstairs in the living room with poor, patient Tor, stuck in front of a video we'd rented: *Shrek*. I'm sure Auntie Pauline and Uncle Joe were hoping me and Rowan would be doing something more educational with the twins while we were spending the day baby-sitting them (hey, so much for Auntie Pauline and Uncle Joe babysitting *us*!), but by 2 p.m. we'd had enough – there's only so much whining, screaming and staring you can take from a couple of alien elves. So it was a quick stroll up to the video shop on Park Road, and that was me and Rowan off the hook for a bit this afternoon.

Well, we were doing our best, which you could tell wasn't what our aunt was looking forward to. Yesterday, when they'd arrived home from their visitations in Guildford and Grandma had headed home, Auntie Pauline had announced at teatime that she and Uncle Joe wanted to have a day shopping for souvenirs together in the West End today. Linn, Ro, me and Tor looked at our aunt and uncle blankly, not really sure what Auntie Pauline was getting at. Then Uncle Joe had turned to Linn and said, "How about it? Babysitting, I mean! You're not working tomorrow, are you, Linnhe?"

It was a bit rich of them to ask Linn for a favour, considering they'd just hijacked her precious, perfectly kept room for their monster son (Dad had called her on her mobile at the shop where she works to warn her that Charlie was moving in). Auntie Pauline and Uncle Joe might have noticed she was less than thrilled about it if they'd had the brains to see that she'd been sitting stony-faced and silent all through tea. But then Auntie Pauline and Uncle Joe's minds weren't programmed to spot other people's feelings. So they charged right in and asked her anyway, thinking – I suppose – that because Linn is seventeen, pretty and hyper-neat, she was the obvious choice to look after the brats. Sorry – *twins*. Fortunately for our aunt and uncle, Linn was too polite a person to growl "no" at them, but *unfortunately* for my aunt and uncle, she explained that her shifts at work had changed at the last minute, so they'd reluctantly ended up turning to crimped-haired, tie-dyed, tattoo-wearing Ro, who definitely (and unfortunately) *did* have a day off from her hectic schedule of sweeping and mug-washing at the hairdresser's. With irresponsible, off-the-rails *me* as back-up.

Wow, my aunt and uncle must *really* have been desperate to buy those novelty *I* ❤ *London* tea towels for the folks back home if they were willing to entrust Carli and Charlie into our exclusive care...

"God, Ro – your hair is getting *so* dark!" I said, unable to avoid the sheeny-shiny glare of the mahogany-brown head bowed down in front of me.

"Yeah? D'you think?" Rowan gazed up at me, with a huge smile on her face, as if I'd given her some massive compliment or something. "But do you reckon Grandma's noticed?"

Did I think Grandma had *noticed*? Grandma had done nothing but stare at Rowan – eyebrows furrowed – across the kitchen table the last few times she'd come for tea. And no wonder, Ro's hair had miraculously gone from boring mid-brown to glossy chestnut to browny-black in double-quick time. How could she possibly think Grandma wouldn't catch on?

Not that I was going to point *any* of that out to Rowan at this precise time. After yesterday's horrid flare-up with her, all I wanted was for Ro and I to be the best buddies that an airhead and her easily stressed sister ever could be.

"I dunno..." I shrugged, not totally capable of a

full-on "no" – i.e. a lie. "But I've been meaning to ask…"

Ro smiled up at me, as questioning and innocent as could be.

"…all these fake tattoos you've been sticking on. Is that like the hair? Are you trying to get Grandma used to that too?"

I've never seen Rowan go so pale as she did right then. If I'd held a glass of milk right up against her face, you wouldn't have been able to spot the difference (er … apart from the fact that a glass of milk doesn't have two eyes, a nose and a mouth on it, of course).

"Don't tell, Ally!"

I gulped, staring hard at the blank space on Rowan's arm that had so recently played host to the rose-circled heart, the huge leopard and the fat cupid. There was – phew! – nothing there but pinky-white skin. For the moment.

"What are you on about?" I asked her, hoping – *praying* – she wasn't planning a skull and cross-bones emblem any time soon.

"I really, really want a proper tattoo, Al, but I can't decide what it should be! That's why I've been trying out loads of fakes, just to see what looks good. That, and like you say, trying to get Grandma less shocked by the idea…"

Urgh ... what was Rowan thinking? That she'd lure our gran into a false sense of security and then wait till she was twenty-five and admit that the vision of the Grim Reaper on a motorcycle that had been on her arm for the last ten years hadn't been a wash-off tattoo *after* all?

While my mind whirred, the cats in my lap stirred; both raising their heads and staring curiously towards the door. At first, I couldn't make out anything – and you know what cats are like, they enjoy freaking you out by staring earnestly at the wall as if they can see spooky spirits *you* can't.

And *then* I heard the wonky floorboard outside on the landing give one of its squelchy, farty squeaks.

"What's that?" Ro's head spun round.

For a second, all four of us – me, Ro, Eddie and Derek – held our breaths. And then the door was suddenly head-butted open, and Rolf came skulking into the room, looking sheepish as he headed straight under Rowan's bed. The only thing that stopped him flattening himself to the floor and wriggling completely under it was the three big, plastic plant pots that were tied to his tail with some gardening twine.

Was that the work of some strange poltergeist?

Or perhaps some mysterious, malevolent, missing tortoise? Well, it *had* to be Spartacus, didn't it? There was no *way* my cousin Charlie could have been involved in anything so mean. Oh, no. Not where an animal was concerned.

Ahem.

Um, did my nose just grow to Pinocchio proportions there…?

Chapter 17

BISCUITS AND SYMPATHY

Tor's library books were overdue.

That's the excuse me and Rowan gave Uncle Joe and Auntie Pauline when they arrived back home from their souvenir-buying shopping trip at four o'clock today. They seemed to swallow it, though why they thought it took me *and* Ro to escort Tor and his one copy of *The Secret World of Squirrels* to the local library I don't know. But we didn't care; babysitting Carli and Charlie had been bad enough, but when Auntie Pauline started moaning about Oxford Street and London in general (again) and Uncle Joe burst out laughing at the sight of us untangling twine and flower pots from Rolf's tail, we'd had enough. Me, Tor and Rowan needed an excuse to get out and get out *fast*.

Naturally, we didn't *really* have to go to the library. In fact, we didn't go at all. Once we got outside our front door, we turned in the opposite direction and skedaddled to Grandma's as fast as our fourteen legs would carry us (Winslet and Rolf had joined us for the great escape).

We didn't know for sure that Grandma would be in, but we'd taken the spare key she always left at our place. If she was home, then fine – we'd just tell her we were taking the dogs out for a walk and thought we'd drop by, and even if she wasn't around to personally dole out biscuits herself, we knew she wouldn't mind if we raided the biscuit box, as long as we cleared up our crumbs before we left. And with Rolf and Winslet around, that wouldn't be a problem.

"Hello?"

Something was wrong with the intercom today; you could hardly make out Grandma's voice above the scratchy electronic whines.

"It's us!" I shouted back into the silver box, hoping Grandma could hear us better than we could hear her.

She must have: the buzzer sounded, the automatic door-lock clicked open and we all hurried inside.

"Hope she doesn't ask us how we're getting on with Uncle Joe and that lot," said Ro, slipping the unused spare key back in her pocket as we all bounded up the stairs.

"Hope she's got Hobnobs!" Tor chipped in,

looking chirpier than he had in days (twelve days to be precise).

As we approached the door to Grandma's flat, it was pulled open ... by Linn.

"What are you doing here?" Rowan frowned at her.

"I'm staying here, remember?"

Linn might be acting defiant, but her pale cheeks were telltale pink. And well they might be. So much for her shifts at the shop changing at the last minute. If she wasn't having a day off then I was a duck-billed platypus (and I'm not, just in case you were wondering).

"You told Auntie Pauline and Uncle Joe you were working today, and that's why you couldn't babysit!" I narrowed my eyes at her, knowing she was marginally less likely to argue with me than Ro.

Linn stood tall and together in the doorway, a smart reply just about to spill from her lips. And then her shoulders sank and she got real.

"God, I'm sorry. I just couldn't *bear* the thought of babysitting. Especially not after they persuaded Dad to let that *boy* invade my room..."

Five minutes and forty-five seconds later, there was only one broken Hobnob left at the bottom of the packet.

"Go on, Tor!" I smiled, passing him the rustling plastic packet.

Yep, me and my sisters loved Tor enough to give him the last (half a) biscuit, but then it's easy to be generous when you've already eaten so many so quickly that you feel slightly sick.

"I'm telling you, Linnhe, if Auntie Pauline tells me *one* more time that I could be as pretty as you if only I tried harder, I'll scream so loud that she'll have permanent tinnitus!"

"Tinny-who?" Tor asked Rowan, while he busied himself splitting his half a biscuit into four pieces (a bit for him, a bit each for Rolf and Winslet, a bit for Grandma's kitten Mushu who was currently curling himself like a slinky Siamese scarf around Linn's shoulders).

"Ringing sound in your ears," Linn explained quickly, before turning back to Rowan (and making Mushu dig his mini-claws in to keep his balance). "God, is she *still* doing that, Ro? It makes me totally *cringe* every time Auntie Pauline starts with that stuff!"

"Not your fault," Rowan shrugged, making the procession of fairies on her arm flutter prettily (she'd used practically the whole packet of tattoos in one go).

For a second, I wished a documentary crew

from the BBC could be in the room with us, just to record this moment for posterity. David Attenborough could be crouched behind the sofa, whispering, "Look... Linn and Rowan Love getting on well – we're very privileged to witness such a rare event. It's only happened twice in the last millennium, and both in the same week!" into his microphone.

"I *know* it's not my fault, but it still creeps me out the way her and Uncle Joe keep going on about 'how pretty' I am, and how much I look like Mum – and then slagging her off!"

"At least Uncle Joe hasn't accused *you* of being 'off the rails'," I pointed out to Linn, as I carefully brushed the crumbs off the table into my hand (like us off-the-rails, delinquent children do).

Rolf opened his mouth right on cue and let me deposit the crumbs neatly into his waiting gob.

"God, is Uncle Joe blind or something?" Linn exclaimed. "Hasn't he *noticed* that his own kids are horrid, spoilt little monsters?"

"Course he hasn't! He's been too busy hitting Dad."

I meant that wryly, but it made all of us quiet for a minute, thinking of all the arm-thumping and oh-so-funny remarks Uncle Joe had constantly flung Dad's way through this entire visit (at least Dad was getting a chance for the bruises to fade while he was away at the bike fair). It was always meant to be taken as cheery banter – after all, Uncle Joe never stopped grinning and laughing – but somehow the arm-thumping and back-slapping had a habit of being that *bit* too forceful and the oh-so-funny remarks tended to come across like oh-so-snidey digs.

"So, what's Grandma been saying?" I broke the silence and asked Linn. "Does she still think the Relatives From Hell are OK? Has she said anything since Sunday?"

"What happened on Sunday?" Tor squinted at me.

"Nothing," said me, Linn and Rowan in unison.

"Anyway, no – Grandma hasn't said anything," Linn carried on. "But she can't stand them!"

"But if she hasn't said anything, how do you *know* she can't stand them? It didn't sound like that when she was telling us off!" said Rowan.

"Telling you off about what?" Tor asked.

"Nothing important," Linn told him, then peeled Mushu off her shoulders and passed him to Tor to shut him up. "Anyway, you know how Grandma is – she's too polite to say things out loud, but you just *know*."

Grandma is polite. In fact, she's so well-mannered that she once told a mugger to have patience when he yelled at her to hurry up and hand over her pension money outside the post office. When he just yelled some more, she told him he wasn't going to get anywhere by being so rude. But even Grandma can get pushed to the edge: the third time he yelled at her, she let fly with her shopping bag full of King Edward potatoes and knocked him right out. Her picture was even on the front of the *Hornsey Journal*.

"Know how?" I pushed Linn.

"Well, you just have to look at the way she purses her lips when any of them start up," Linn continued.

Hmm. I made a mental note to watch Grandma's face more closely in future. But there was something *else* that had occurred to me; a weird thought that had wafted through my head loads of times over the last week or two.

"Um … do you think Dad actually *likes* Uncle Joe?" I found myself asking aloud.

The four of us all exchanged glances for a second (so did Rolf – I think he was hoping we were discussing the benefits of breaking open another packet of biscuits).

"I don't know if Dad *likes* him, exactly," said Linn, after giving my question her consideration. "But he's his brother, so I guess he does love him."

I looked around at my sisters and brother and realized how lucky I was compared to Dad – I didn't just love my family, I really liked them too.

And I liked and loved my dad so much that I knew I owed it to him to try a *little* bit harder to get on with our Relatives From Hell for just a *little* while longer. We all did.

From underneath the table, Winslet let out a long, low growl, as if she could read my mind, and didn't approve one little bit...

THINK OF DAD, THINK OF DAD, THINK OF DAD...

"Aw, go on – *please* come round, Sandie. We need help!"

It was Friday, Spartacus had been missing since last Sunday evening and Tor was now bordering on *frantic*.

Me and him – the only ones at home this morning – were turning the house upside-down in search of the vanishing tortoise. We were having no luck ... there were no trails of lettuce to lead us to his hiding place; and we didn't have any access to infrared, heat-sensitive tortoise-tracking radar devices either. (Maybe they'd have them in Woollies, though – right next to the warp-factor, electron neutralizing atomic alien vaporizers...)

No, what we needed was another pair of helping hands in the hunt before Tor was forced to stick a "Lost" poster up around the neighbourhood and confess to Michael the vet that we'd managed to mislay his client's much-loved pet.

Urgh...

"Ally, I really like Tor and everything," Sandie mumbled down the phone, "and it's a real shame Spartacus is still missing, but I'm sorry – I, um, *can't*."

"*Why* can't you?" I pushed her.

"Er ... it's just that I promised Mum I'd help her ... help her do ... um..."

"You, Sandie Walker, are the world's worst liar."

"Sorry..."

"*You* just don't want to come round to my house in case you bump into any of my relatives, do you?"

"Well ... yeah."

I'd just done one of those dumb things again, hadn't I? Same as when I tried to persuade Rowan to have Carli stay in her room *right* after I'd gone and told her what the little troll was up to. And I hadn't learned my lesson – Sandie phones for a catch-up chat; *I* waffle on endlessly about how awful the Relatives From Hell have been since we last spoke, and then I expect her to want to come round here and hang out with them.

"But they won't be back for ages yet!" I tried to lure her. "They've gone out for a drive; Auntie Pauline and Uncle Joe want to show my cousins the places and landmarks near where they grew up!"

It would serve my aunt and uncle right if Carli and Charlie were just as annoyingly disinterested in that as they were in anything else London had to offer. Actually, the only things they seemed to have liked in the whole time they'd been here was the games arcade in the Trocadero ("Still not as good as Dave and Busters arcade back in Toronto!") and Dunkin' Donuts.

As a big fan of Dunkin' Donuts myself (specially the doughnuts that come with the multicoloured sprinkles), I can understand the appeal, but if you think *that's* better than the London Dungeon ("Not scary enough!"), Madame Tussauds ("Boring!") and the Planetarium ("Who cares about stupid stars?"), then you need your little elf head examined...

"Um, I'm still not coming, Ally."

"Don't blame you," I shrugged to myself. "Hey, did I tell you this thing me and my sisters and Tor came up with yesterday?"

"No – what thing?"

It was a "coping mechanism"; that was what Linn called it (you can tell she's studying psychology, can't you?). Basically, round at Grandma's, me and Love Children numbers 1, 2 and 4 were all talking about ways of *not* letting the Relatives From Hell wind us up. I told them I'd been doing the old "Counting to Ten" thing, only it wasn't really working. But that definitely got Linn's mind whirring.

"When they bug us, we're all going to say, 'Think of Dad, think of Dad, think of Dad...' over and over in our heads till we stop being so annoyed," I explained to Sandie.

"Oh, that's nice."

Sandie didn't sound too impressed, but then I guess it made more sense to me and my strung-out family.

"*Alleeeeeeeeeeee! Come and help!*" a distant voice drifted through from the vicinity of the garden.

"That's Tor. Got to go – neglecting my search and rescue duties," I hurriedly told Sandie.

"Why don't you set up lettuce traps around the house? You know, try and tempt the tortoise out from wherever it's hiding?" Sandie suggested hastily, before I had a chance to hang up.

"Because," I sighed, "we happen to have a canine hoover in the house called Rolf who isn't fussy about what he eats, as long as it's food."

And with that, I said my goodbyes to Sandie, pulled my soggy trainer lace out of Rolf's gently-chewing mouth, and went out to the garden to see how frazzled my little brother had become by now...

Several hours, the return of the Relatives From Hell, and no tortoise later, I went to walk upstairs and was practically sent flying by a blur of four fast, black and white cats and a slower, hopping, ginger one zooming down towards me.

What's up with them? I wondered, as my ankles were softly brushed by a flurry of static fur.

I stared up to see what had got the cats so spooked, and heard the predictable thunder of elfin feet. But as soon as Charlie whipped down the attic stairs from Linn's room on to the landing and saw me, he slowed to a standstill, hiding the egg whisk I'd just caught a glimpse of behind his back.

"What are you doing?" I asked, as Charlie pretended to examine the bannister and sauntered down towards me.

"Nothing…" he said innocently.

"Well, you won't be needing that, then," I told him, grabbing the egg whisk from his hand as I continued past him on my way to the loo.

Think of Dad, think of Dad, think of Dad, think of Dad…

The living-room door thunked as Charlie disappeared in there, and I sincerely hoped none of the cats had chosen that room to hide in. Then just as I was about to nip into the bathroom, I could make out noises coming from Dad's room. Rattles and thunks, to be precise. The rattle and thunk of coat hangers clinking and drawers being opened and shut.

Erm, what exactly was going on in there?

"Oh, hello, Ally!" Auntie Pauline glanced cheerfully over at me, then turned back to the long, floaty, hippy dress she was holding up.

Behind her on the bed was a pile of other floaty, hippy clothes and a mound of the hand-knitted, chunky, woolly cardies Mum loved to wear.

"That's Mum's..." I said stupidly. (Well, it wasn't exactly *Dad*'s – none of it was his size.)

"I know, dear," said Auntie Pauline matter-of-factly.

"What are you doing with them?" I asked her, feeling my blood go from frozen to boiling point in the space of two seconds.

My God, the cheek of her! Just 'cause she was sleeping in this room, it didn't give her the right to rummage around and try my mum's clothes on!

"Having a clear-out."

Urgh, this was *worse* than simply trying Mum's clothes on...

"A ... a *what*?"

"Now don't get like *that*, Ally," my aunt raised her eyebrows in warning at me. "I'm just trying to help your father out, here! I know he'd find it too traumatic to throw your mother's things away, so I thought I'd make a start on it for him. And it's for the best, after all – it's about time your father admitted to himself that Melanie's not coming home after all these years!"

If I was the heroine in *Crouching Tiger, Hidden Dragon* (a film that Tor was pretty disappointed in, by the way – he expected to see more actual tigers and dragons in it than people kicking each other in trees), I'd have leapt through the air right now, expertly kick-boxed my aunt out of the way, and grabbed my mum's dress out of her hand before she'd even reached the ground.

But I wasn't the heroine in *Crouching Tiger, Hidden Dragon*; I was Ally Love from Crouch End and the only thing I could do right then was to get out of the room before I gave my stupid aunt the satisfaction of seeing tears in my eyes.

"Of course, I'll chat to your father first, and see which charity he'd prefer these to go to..."

Think of Dad, think of Dad, think of Dad, think of Dad... I whispered silently in my head as I bolted for the attic stairs.

"Oh, Ally! I'm only talking about a few *clothes*, for goodness' sake!"

...think of Dad, think of Dad, think of Dad, think of Dad...

But as I slammed my bedroom door shut and

leant hard against it, the only image I had in my head was of Mum, Mum, Mum...

Chapter 19

FIREWORKS AND FREAK-OUTS

I'm a *big* fan of classical music.

Ha, ha, only joking.

I may know nothing about Bach and those other blokies (no matter *how* much our music teacher tries to get us into it), but what I *do* know is that in the summertime, a Saturday night at Kenwood House in Hampstead Heath is brilliant fun.

For a start, Hampstead Heath is great: it's this huge, huge, *huge* park in the north of London, not very far from Crouch End. It's not a fountain-and-bandstand kind of park; it's more like miles and miles of wild woods, little lakes and meadows stuck right in the middle (ish) of the city. And if you were looking at a diagram of the Heath, at the very top of it is this fancy white Georgian mansion thing. This is Kenwood House, which was once owned by some rich guy (Mr Kenwood?) who used to have the whole of the heath as his back garden a couple of hundred years ago (easy to lose a tortoise in *that*).

Anyway, Mr Kenwood's big back garden is now

open to anyone and everyone. And someone sometime decided it would be kind of nice to do open-air classical concerts on summer Saturday nights at this lake right by Kenwood. The way it works is, if you're really hot on violins and stuff, you pay money to go and sit in this snoot enclosure right in front of the band – sorry, orchestra. But if you're everyone else (and there are thousands of everyone else's) you sit on the rolling grassy banks beside Kenwood House, half-listening to the music drifting over, but spending more time yakking, lazing, eating late-night picnics, playing late-night Frisbee and having a laugh as the sun sets, and waiting for the sky to go dark so you can cheer on the fireworks that always finish the end of the night. See what I mean about not having to know anything about classical stuff?

Kenwood concerts are legendary in London and everyone who goes to them (even if they're more into the Stereophonics or the Teletubbies than Vivaldi) loves them. *Except* for this one old actor bloke who lives nearby; Dad says he used to play a grumpy old man on a telly series in the 1960s, and he seems to have kept in character in real life too, 'cause he's spent years writing in to the local papers about how noisy and horrible the concerts are and how they should be banned. Um, excuse me … but it's not exactly as noisy as living under the flight path to Heathrow and hearing planes rumble over your head every five seconds or something, night and day, is it? Course, there're always people who want to put a downer on something that everyone else is enjoying…

"Is this grass damp?" frowned Auntie Pauline, wriggling her bum around on one of the three travel rugs we'd spread on the grass to accommodate the Love clan gathering, on this last night before the Canadian branch of the family flew homewards. (No cheering at the back now.)

"It hasn't rained in the last three weeks, so I shouldn't think so!" Dad said cheerfully, as he helped himself to another chicken drumstick out of the many plastic tubs of food we'd brought along with us tonight. (All Grandma's handiwork, since Dad had only got back from the bike fair this afternoon.)

"Well, it feels damp to me," Auntie Pauline said sniffily.

"Maybe you're like one of those water-diviner people, who can find water wherever they go!" said Grandma's boyfriend Stanley, cheerfully raising his white eyebrows as he spoke. "You know how it is; some people have real talent for putting a dampener on things…"

Was that a hint of a smile on Grandma's pursed lips? It was hard to tell in this darkened, lamplit light. She was watching (pretending to watch?) Tor scooting around the other blankets-worth of picnickers with his helium Tigger balloon, so it was hard to be sure.

"More wine, Joe? Pauline?" Dad asked, holding out a bottle, with what looked suspiciously like a smirk on his face too. Or maybe he was just happy. It was hard to work out what exactly was going on with Dad at the moment; I couldn't wait till we had him all to ourselves again. (Not long now...)

Speaking of not knowing what was going on, something pretty funny happened last night: I pretended I felt sick and didn't come down to tea (I was frantically – and vainly – trying to formulate a plan to rescue Mum's clothes and couldn't bear to watch Auntie Pauline stuffing her face in the kitchen, having built up an appetite *meddling*). But *that* wasn't the funny thing. Once it got late, after I'd watched – through barely opened eyes – Carli slip into my bed and head off to snoozeland, I decided to tiptoe down to the kitchen as if I was on the hunt for a sneaky glass of milk or whatever I could find in the fridge. I didn't know what time it was exactly, but everyone under the age of thirty-nine seemed to be asleep, while everyone forty and above (i.e. Uncle Joe and Auntie Pauline) could be heard chatting in the living room. So I nipped into Dad's room, with some vague idea about dragging all the bags downstairs and stashing them in the garden shed for safety (yeah, *that* was going to be easy to do silently, I *don't* think). But the thing was, there were *no* black bags or bundles of woollies on the bed any more. In fact, on closer inspection, every woolly cardie and hippy dress was back in its place, back where it always was. How spooky was that? Had Auntie Pauline had a change of heart? (I doubted it.) Then what had happened? Who knew...? All *I* knew was that I immediately felt a thousand times better for seeing those floaty bits hanging up in Dad's wardrobe again...

"It's ridiculous that they put a band on and you can't see 'em!" Uncle Joe announced, holding his plastic cup out to Dad and peering off at the pin-prick orchestra by the lake.

"Yeah, but that isn't the point, is it?" said Dad breezily, trying to ignore the fact that Charlie was currently drizzling drips out of his Ribena carton on to the flickering garden candle we'd brought along with us.

"Careful!" Linn smiled brightly, while roughly grabbing the carton out of our cousin's hand. "You don't want to put the flame out, or splash boiling hot wax on yourself, do you, Charlie!"

Coming along to Kenwood tonight was a brilliant idea on Dad's part; a much nicer, more personal farewell dinner than heading for the nearest pizza restaurant. Not that anyone amongst The Other Loves seemed to appreciate that. So far, Auntie Pauline had moaned about the busy roads on the way here, the lack of parking, the lack of salt in Grandma's home-made potato salad, the queues at the loos and much, much more too miserably moany to report. Uncle Joe had moaned – with an inane grin on his face – about Dad's directions to the Heath, about the splendid view of London from up here on the hill at Kenwood being partly obscured by trees ("They should chop 'em down!"), and about how far away the orchestra was, i.e. the one that we were listening to for *free*. Meanwhile, the elf twins whined endlessly about how bored they were, then entertained themselves by asking "Is it time to go home yet?" over and over again (Carli), and making neighbouring babies and toddlers cry hysterically (Charlie, wearing the gorilla mask he'd bought at the zoo and growling menacingly).

Not long now, not long now, not long now... I told myself silently, quietly delirious that in approximately fifteen hours' time, my Relatives From Hell would be packing themselves into their hire car and heading back to Heathrow. (Should I phone the Canadian Embassy now and warn them?)

No matter how obnoxious Auntie Pauline, Uncle Joe, Carli and Charlie were, I could stand it. Specially when we were all here – me, Dad, Linn, Rowan, Tor, Grandma and Stanley. The Other Loves – The Horrible Loves – were outnumbered. We were invincible: nothing they said could bother us.

"Mummy…" said Carli, in her best, babyish voice, as she laid her head on her mother's shoulders.

Oh, here we go again, I thought. *"Is it time to go home yet?"* I wished the fireworks would hurry up and start so the noise would drown my cousin out.

"What, sweetie pie?" Auntie Pauline asked, wriggling her jacket under her bottom to protect it from the make-believe damp.

"Rowan's a *bad* girl. She tells *lies*…"

As the words tripped off Carli's telltale lips, everything seemed to stop mid-air – like it was freeze-framed on a DVD. (A DVD like Chloe's got; back at Palace Heights Road all we have is a prehistoric, thousand-year-old video, where you press freeze-frame and the whole machine starts juddering and spluttering, finally spitting out the tape after you've got motion sickness watching the stalled scene flicker at fit-inducing speeds in front of you.)

"What do you mean, Carli?" her mother frowned at her, which is what the rest of us were doing too – especially a stunned Rowan.

"I heard her and Ally *whispering*, and Rowan says she's going to get a *real* tattoo, even though she'd promised her gran that she wouldn't. That's wrong, isn't it, Mummy?"

Ahhh … so the other day when me and Ro were reluctantly babysitting; that squeak outside the door *wasn't* just poor old Rolf, come to show us his latest humiliation. Carli had obviously been hovering out there by the wonky floorboard, desperately trying to earwig on us.

"Uh-oh! Got a bit of a wild child on your hands there, Martin! No guesses who *she* takes after – and it's not you, soft lad!" Uncle Joe laughed uproariously at his own non-joke, and gave Dad a quick punch on the arm while he was at it.

"Oh, I think you might have picked things up a bit wrong, Carli," Dad smiled at my cousin, while blanking Uncle Joe. "Rowan's not going to get a *real* tattoo. For a start, she's not old enough to have one done. Are you, Ro?"

But Rowan didn't answer – the expression on

her face read stunned, shocked and … guilty. And the fact that she suddenly tugged the sleeve of her T-shirt further down her arm was a real giveaway too.

"Let me see," Grandma said firmly, in the same I'm-not-having-any-nonsense voice that she used when any of us came whimpering to her with a splinter in our finger or a bee sting on our leg.

In a nanosecond, our gran had flipped up Ro's sleeve to reveal one pretty huge white dressing.

Good grief … she'd done it for real.

Me and Linn swapped tense glances; what had Rowan gone and slapped *permanently* on her arm? Knowing our sister, it could be anything from a whole school of dolphins to the entire cast of her all-time favourite film, *The Wizard Of Oz*…

Grandma gave Ro a cool stare over the top of her glasses. "May I see what you've done, please?"

Ooh, that school teacher voice; that wasn't a good sign. Grandma was mad as hell. Rowan was in so much trouble. And from the matching smirks on Carli and Auntie Pauline's faces, they were loving every minute of it.

"This guy Jake at work did it yesterday," Rowan began to chatter nervously, while wincing as she slowly peeled the sticky dressing off. "He does tattoos and piercings through the back three days a week. I think he thinks I'm eighteen, and I've never bothered to tell him I'm not…"

With one last tug and a grimace, Rowan pulled the dressing away, revealing … a scab. A very *small* scab.

"What's it supposed to *be*?" asked Linn, leaning closer and squinting.

In an effort to be vaguely useful, I lifted the garden candle into the air, wafting it closer to Rowan's arm.

"It's a…"

"…ladybird!" Tor exclaimed, his Tigger balloon bobbing in the evening breeze.

And so it was. Under the healing, crusty bit of dried blood (bleurgh) you could just make out a little red circle with tiny black dots. A life-sized ladybird; i.e. so weeny, you could mistake it for a freckle with a suntan.

"Yeah – I got the idea from that photo of us at Michael and Harry's barbecue. You remember, Ally? The one when the ladybird landed on my arm?"

"That exact spot!" Tor giggled delightedly, sticking his finger into Ro's skin and making her wince again. "Ooh, sorry!"

"Well, young lady," Auntie Pauline suddenly butted in. "I'm hearing excuses, but I'm not hearing any apologies. And quite frankly—"

"Quite *frankly*, Pauline," Grandma growled, in her *sternest* headteacher way, "I'd appreciate it if you kept your opinion to yourself for once!"

Yikes.

Everyone – including Dad, Uncle Joe and Stanley – looked gobsmacked. Meanwhile, even in the semi-darkness, it was plain to see that Auntie Pauline had gone beetroot.

"I'm only trying to—"

"Interfere," Grandma said bluntly, giving Auntie Pauline a cool stare.

"But she's a fifteen-year-old child, for goodness' sake, and she's *plainly* out of control, if she's going against your wishes and scarring herself with this *awful* thing!"

"It's not awful, it's very nice. Or at least it will be, once it heals. Here, Rowan – put your dressing back on, please."

Rowan did as Grandma ordered her, mute with shock at Grandma sticking up for her – *and* her tattoo.

"Now, listen here," Uncle Joe began blustering. "*No one* talks to my wife like that. Martin, are you going to let her talk to my wife like that?"

"Yes."

"*What?*" bellowed Uncle Joe.

"I said, yes!" Dad repeated more forcefully, his face looking taut and tense in the candlelight. "Because no one gets to talk to *my* family like that!"

Around us, I could see other picnickers tuning in to our own family fireworks instead of the real ones that had just begun blasting above us.

"Well, if *you're* happy to have children that show you no respect," Uncle Joe shrugged. "Mind you, that's no surprise when your own wife hasn't shown you any respect by *waltzing* off around the world and—"

"Joe, the only people showing me no respect are you and your family," said Dad firmly. "I ask you to get your boy to stop upsetting mine, and you carry on encouraging him to misbehave. I ask you not to bad-mouth my wife in front of the children, and you do it anyway. I ask Pauline not to mess around with things in our house, and she still does."

"Auntie Pauline was trying to throw Mum's clothes out yesterday, Dad," Rowan suddenly announced. "I caught her putting them all into plastic rubbish bags. I told her she couldn't do that, but she told me I was just being silly and childish. But I sneaked into your room later on at night and put everything back where it came from!"

So it was Rowan! I didn't know she'd come across Auntie Pauline doing that too! But then I'd been too busy moping on my own up in the attic.

"So it was you!" squeaked Auntie Pauline, shooting daggers at Ro. "Do you realize that I spent *hours* trying to sort all that out as a favour to your father! I knew he'd be too upset to get round to doing it himself!"

"Pauline!" Dad burst out, his normally calm face now twitching with rage. "How *dare* you go through Melanie's things without asking permission? And speaking of that, I don't remember your daughter asking anyone's permission to wear one of my wife's necklaces!"

Our heads – all rattling with snaps, crackles and pops at this sudden flare-up – spun round to stare at Carli. Sure enough, peeking out from the top of her sweatshirt was a jade necklace that normally hung along with others on an old wooden mug tree on the dressing table in Dad's room. So ... it wasn't just *my* room she liked to sneakily rummage around in.

"I was going to put it back, Daddy!" Carli whined, turning on the waterworks, and fingering the necklace with her mauve-painted nails.

Uncle Joe went purple, but instead of telling Carli off, he blasted at my dad some more.

"You know your trouble, Martin?" he glared. "You're jealous. Just 'cause *some* of us have made successful lives for ourselves! And look at you – you're struggling to bring up your kids alone in that terrible old house, running that no-hope bike shop. You don't ... you don't even have a car!"

I swear, by the look on her face, if Grandma had had a shopping bag full of King Edwards handy, she'd have walloped it straight in Uncle Joe's blubbery belly after that stupid comment, same as she did to the mugger, months ago.

"And *you* don't have any manners," Grandma burst in. "You're nothing but a big bully, Joe Love!"

I nearly jumped when the people sitting on the next rug to us burst into a spontaneous round of applause.

Maybe it would have been sort of inappropriate for Grandma to stand up and take a bow, but all the same, she was my hero. She might have been sixty-something, but she was still tough enough to take on Uncle Joe, *easy*.

Do they do WWF granny-wrestling competitions...? I couldn't help wondering. She'd beat all contestants, no problem.

Go, Grandma! Go, Grandma! Go, Grandma!

PEACE, QUIET AND MACARONI...

As the hire car pulled away from the pavement and began picking up speed, I was vaguely aware of Linn holding something in the opposite hand from the one she was waving.

At first I thought it might be a small bottle of bleach – I knew she was planning to strip and fumigate her room the second Charlie had vacated the premises...

"What's that?" I asked, my own hand busy waving too.

We were all there – Dad, me, Linn, Rowan and Tor – all politely seeing the Relatives From Hell off on their homeward journey.

"I'm not *proud* of my outburst, you know," Grandma had told me and my *distinctly* proud brother and sisters last night on the way home in Stanley's car. (Dad had shared a stony, silent journey home with The Other Loves.) "And I'm asking you all to be *very* grown-up and act pleasant and civilized to your aunt and uncle and cousins till they leave tomorrow." And that's what we were doing; acting pleasant and civilized, even though we'd just seen Carli stick her pointy little tongue out at us as the car pulled away. I won't even *tell* you what Charlie was doing. I felt warm inside anyway; just knowing that Grandma understood what we'd been going through was good enough for me. Her *and* Dad.

"Parting shot from Charlie – found it holding Britney's beak shut," Linn answered me, holding out a plastic clothes peg.

"Britney!" Tor gasped, and immediately left our farewell party on the doorstep for the back garden, to comfort and coo over his victimized pet pigeon.

As the car finally slipped around the corner, Rowan immediately punched the air and whooped – and just as immediately regretted it when it hurt her healing arm.

"You're not upset, are you, Dad?" I asked, noticing him still staring off in the direction of the now-disappeared car.

"How do you mean, Ally Pally?" he gazed down at me.

"Well, you wanted to get closer to Uncle Joe, and instead you ended up falling out with him!"

"The truth of it is, Ally," Dad sighed, after a second's pause, "somehow, me and your uncle were never close, even as kids. So I guess I'm a bit sad, but not really surprised, that we still don't get on, even at this age."

"Was he always bossing you around, even when you were little?" asked Linn disapprovingly, which was pretty funny coming from someone who could be the Queen of Bossiness herself. (But at least she wasn't mean with it. Well, not *properly* mean. And she never hit any of us – even Rowan, even *after* eating one of her spectacularly bad meals.)

"Yeah, he did, and he was always your granny Love's favourite, so he tended to get away with it," Dad explained. "But that's the funny thing about families – just 'cause you're related, it doesn't mean you get to act any way you want to, and expect people to put up with it. It's the same as with friends, you've got to earn the love of your brothers and sisters."

I felt a bit funny when he said that – it sounded so slushy that it kind of made me feel embarrassed and choked up all at once. And then I noticed how totally *sheepish* my two sisters were looking.

"That dressing on your arm, Ro: look how dirty it is – that's disgusting," Linn suddenly announced to Rowan.

Ro peered round at the decidedly grimy white dressing on her upper arm and frowned.

"I think there's still some big Winnie-the-Pooh plasters left over, from when Tor scraped his knee playing Hide and Seek with Rolf," Linn continued. "I could put one of those on for you, *if* you wanted…"

"OK," Rowan shrugged, and sealed the current truce between my bickering sisters. (At least Dad and Uncle's Joe's rubbish relationship did *some* good. And who knows? Linn and Rowan's truce could last all the way to … next Tuesday!)

"*Allleeeeeee! Daaadd!* Come and see what Sandie found!"

All of us turned and hurried into the house, towards the garden and the sound of Tor's voice, nearly tripping over Sandie's big bag cluttering up half the hallway. (Oh, yes, she'd arrived for her postponed week staying with us, even though she had no real reason to, since her own house was papered, painted and totally back to normal. But that was fine by me.)

"Sandie saw him under the shed! He must have been hiding there all this time!" said Tor excitedly pointing to Spartacus, who Sandie was very proudly holding aloft.

"I lured him out with lettuce," she beamed. "But, hey, check this out!"

She spun Spartacus around, sending his four

scaly legs flailing out in a wild panic (he probably thought he was about to be superglued to a skateboard or something, the way things had been round at ours since he arrived).

"That's one of mine!" Rowan exclaimed, spotting the fake cupid's arrow and heart tattoo on one side of his shell.

"More of Charlie's handiwork, I guess!" Dad raised his eyebrows.

"Hey!" I gasped, an idea pinging into my head after hearing what Dad just said. "What about turning the house back into El Paradiso today?"

That was the only handiwork *I* wanted to see: Rowan's brilliant, bad taste posters, streamers and plastic flowers.

"Yeah! I'm going to switch on the bananas!" Tor yelped, tearing towards the back door.

"I'll blow up the donkey again!" Dad grinned, stomping after him.

"OK, I'll stick the posters back up on the doors," said Linn, rolling her eyes, "but I want something more glamorous than Iceland for my room, OK?"

"Hey, can you show me how you make those cute windchimes out of forks, Rowan?" Sandie asked, as she laid Spartacus down on the grass and followed my sister towards the house.

"Sure, but first I've got to fix up Croatia – anyone seen the Blu-tack?"

As my family and Sandie disappeared indoors chatting, I lay down on the grass, with my chin on the ground and looked straight into Spartacus's beady black eyes.

"Trust me," I told him, "you'll like it round here, now the place is back to normal."

Ha! Normal? In this house? Who was I kidding?

Anyway, got to go – Rowan's making another sign to hang outside the front door – saying *The Holidays Start Here!* this time – and I promised to run round to the shops for some more macaroni 'cause she's run out. (I know she's an airhead, but if she gives us macaroni and cheese that tastes of glue and paint tonight, she's in *real* trouble.)

Ally :c)

PS Grandma and Rowan did a deal – in return for not flipping out about the tattoo, Rowan had to promise Grandma to quit dyeing her hair. The only hassle is, she used permanent colour instead of wash-in, wash-out stuff, so now it's started growing out, she's got two-tone hair. Which *she* thinks is kind of cool. (Good grief...)

PPS The night after the Relatives From Hell left, me and Sandie held a candlelit vigil out in the garden, especially for the unfortunate citizens of Canada. Our sympathies, Canada – you really don't deserve your nice country spoiled by the terrible twins and their parents. But please, *please* don't send them back...

PPPS Thought For The Day: The person who came up with the phrase "Blood is thicker than water" obviously didn't have an insensitive bully like Uncle Joe in his family. In fact, I think being "family" is more than just being related; it's about always knowing there's someone there on your side, rooting for you... Although Linn might *not* be on my side when she finds out I pretended I didn't see the "Property of Linn Love" Post-it note on her Philadelphia Light and ate the last of it on toast for lunch today. Hmm, maybe there is something to be said for being an only child (i.e. irate sisters can't kill you...).

Mates, Mysteries and Pretty Weird Weirdness

A sneak preview...

"So how come you're really here this early?" I asked Kyra.

Something had to be up. Something was *always* up with Kyra.

"I phoned Salma last night – she said you've got a spell book!" said Kyra, sitting up straight from her slouch and getting straight to the point.

"Well, for a start, it's not *my* book – it's Kellie's – and anyway, it's not like it's a proper spell book: it's just a dumb thing for fun."

The reason I was quick to jump in like that was because I wasn't exactly thrilled about the idea of Tor getting it into his head that one of his sisters really *was* a witch (i.e. me), as opposed to just *dressing* like one (i.e. Rowan). He had enough strange things to have nightmares about, and I didn't want to add the vision of me casting spells to all the tappings and scratchings that were currently giving him goosebumps.

Not that Tor seemed to be listening to Kyra – he was too wrapped up in cutting his toast into tiny squares and feeding the Marmite pieces to something under the table.

"Who *cares* whose book it is?" Kyra shrugged in her usual infuriatingly casual way. "Just give us a look – I really, really need some help with my nonexistent love life…"

"Sam still not phoned yet?" I asked, conveniently forgetting the fact that she was irritating now that we'd touched on some gossip. Sam was this boy she'd met on holiday a couple of weeks ago. After wall-to-wall snogging sessions whenever their parents weren't looking, Kyra thought she was all set to have a tanned and cool boyfriend when she came back to London. But they do say holiday romances never last, and even though Sam only lived in South London, it might as well have been Mars for all the contact she'd had with him.

"*Three* chances, that's all I said I'd give him," Kyra announced dramatically, holding up her fingers for emphasis.

"Kyra, that's six fingers," I nodded towards her

hands. "How many chances did you give him exactly?"

Kyra wrinkled her freckly brown nose and added another finger for good measure.

"You've left *seven* messages on his mobile?"

She nodded slowly, looking sheepish.

"So, *see*? I really need help! Can I get a look at the book, Ally? Please?!"

I glanced over at Tor, who was now spoonfeeding Marmite straight out of the jar and into whoever's waiting jaws were under the table, and decided it was safe to leave him in Kyra's company for the few minutes it would take to get the book from my bedroom and pull on a pair of jeans.

"Try and cheer him up," I whispered above the buzz of the song blasting out on Radio One. "He had a rotten day yesterday."

"No problem!" the queen of shrugs shrugged once more.

"Cheer him up," I'd said.

"No problem!" she'd said.

Ha!

When I walked back into the kitchen I found Kyra leaning over Tor with a frilly-edged sheet draped over her, making very weird growling noises. Oh, no – my mistake – the growling was coming from Winslet under the table, who really, *really* didn't like the frilly apparition too much judging from the way she'd locked her teeth on to the corner of the sheet and was trying to rip it to shreds.

"What's going on?" I frowned.

"I told Kyra about the tapping," Tor jabbered, jumping up from his seat excitedly, "and she says we've got a polterghost!"

"*Geist!* Polter*geist!*" laughed Kyra, hauling the sheet off her head, the wiry curls of her high ponytail springing back into place.

"Kyra!" I hissed, trying to dislocate Winslet's jaws from the sheet so it could be returned to the laundry basket where it belonged. "Don't go telling him spooky stuff like that!"

"Why not? It's just a bit of fun – like that *Lovey-Dovey Spells* book!"

Good grief, did she need it explained in minute detail? It was like this: if the spell worked, the worst that could happen was that your dream boy fell splat-bang hopelessly in love with you (pretty excellent really). If Tor believed the poltergeist theory, then the worst that could happen was that he'd be so freaked out he'd end up sleeping in my bed for the next three *years*.

And that, Kyra Davies, would certainly *not* be fun…

KaReN McComBie

"A funny and talented author"
Books Magazine

Once upon a time (OK, 1990), Karen McCombie jumped in her beat-up car with her boyfriend and a very bad-tempered cat, leaving her native Scotland behind for the bright lights of London and a desk at "J17" magazine. She's lived in London and acted like a teenager ever since.

The fiction bug bit after writing short stories for "Sugar" magazine. Next came a flurry of teen novels, and of course the best-selling "Ally's World" series, set around and named after Alexandra Palace in North London, close to where Karen lives with her husband Tom, little daughter Milly and an assortment of cats.

PS If you want to know more about Karen check out her website at karenmccombie.com. Karen says, "It's sheeny and shiny, furry and, er, funny (in places)! It's everything you could want from a website and a weeny bit more..."

PPS Email us for a **Karen's Club** newsletter at publicity@scholastic.co.uk and keep in touch with Karen!